THE HUNT

BRAD STEVENS

Black Rose Writing | Texas

ISBN: 978-1-68433-128-4
PUBLISHED BY BLACK ROSE WRITING
www.blackrosewriting.com

Printed in the United States of America
Suggested Retail Price (SRP) $17.95

The Hunt is printed in Gentium Basic

In memory of J.

"Now the question is: why do the governments, the almighty and powerful, become more intolerant every day? History is the narrative of the few, making the lives of the many miserable, while using the most unacceptable excuses: difference of sex, language, religion or political ideas."

- Jafar Panahi, 2012.

THE HUNT

BOOK 1

MARA GORKI

(BEFORE THE HUNT)

CHAPTER 1

Mara hadn't left the apartment in almost a fortnight. She'd been writing a new Melissa Valance novel, potentially her best yet, and saw little reason to venture outside. Food could be ordered online or by phone, while Yuke's weekly visits satisfied her desires for sex and companionship. She wouldn't have described herself as agoraphobic, but staying home gave her a sense of security. Today, however, she intended braving London's streets once again, since a respected journalist named Catherine Darden had flown all the way from America to interview her. Mara's novels, with their independent heroine, were routinely banned by the British Board of Fiction Classification - her agent no longer even bothered submitting them - making the U.S. market particularly important. She had agreed to meet Catherine on the South Bank in an hour, and needed to start getting ready. After saving the file she'd been working on, she shut down her computer while taking one last sip of coffee. She washed the mug in the kitchen sink, then wiped both hands on her jeans, finding this commonplace gesture oddly reassuring. Once in the bedroom, she stripped to her underwear before opening the wardrobe and removing several items of uniform. With her usual reluctance, she put on the white blouse, dark tights, and regulation knee-length black skirt. Court shoes completed the mandatory outfit, and though the jacket was optional, she took it anyway as protection against the cold.

On her way to the meeting, she detoured through Charing Cross Road's second-hand bookshops. Mara's living space was dominated by stacks of books, which served as protective buffers between herself and an increasingly harsh reality. New texts were rigorously censored, but those printed before the Paper Publications Act came into force remained legally available, and an embarrassment of riches could be found in the half-a-dozen specialist stores dotting this busy West End street. Browsing the paperbacks, many of them dating back to the twentieth century, Mara decided to buy a battered copy of *The Aging Boy* by Julian Claman, a name unfamiliar to her. She liked rediscovering those long-forgotten writers whose work had ended up in the cheap bins outside Any Amount of Books. Since the till was located inside, dishonest customers could easily have walked off without paying, yet Mara had never seen this happen. Thieves, it seemed, were not big readers. In any case, the owner probably wouldn't have cared, or even noticed, if these virtually worthless items had been stolen. This, it occurred to Mara, might well be the fate of her own literary output. Perhaps her affection for obscure authors resulted from a suspicion that she'd eventually become an obscure author herself.

As she climbed the steps to Hungerford Bridge and crossed the Thames, the wind blew around her ankles, making her think longingly of the warm jeans she had unwillingly discarded. She disliked the way men stared at her stockinged legs, their openly lascivious looks reminding her she was at best a second-class citizen, at worst little more than an object. As a teenager coming to terms with her illegal sexuality, she'd used loose trousers and baggy jumpers as a defence against the male gaze, and had dreaded the arrival of her eighteenth birthday, when, like all women, she would be required to start wearing the rigidly enforced female uniform. Seven years later, she still resented having to put on a skirt whenever she left home.

Descending towards the South Bank, she noticed a girl, perhaps fifteen years old, depositing a coin in the battered pinball machine located under the bridge. After using the spring launcher to propel a steel ball onto the machine's playing field, the girl made no attempt to activate the flippers, instead standing there, arms hanging limply by her sides, staring desultorily at the ball as it approached the outhole and vanished from view. For some reason, this struck Mara as inexpressibly sad.

The moment she entered the British Film Institute's Benugo Bar, among the few places in London where females unaccompanied by men were permitted to drink, a middle-aged woman came over and shook her hand. "Mara Gorki?" enquired the woman in an American-accented voice so full of confidence it caused heads to turn. "I'm Catherine Darden from *New York Review*."

After exchanging pleasantries, they settled down on one of the large sofas, next to which Catherine positioned the suitcase she had with her. "I'm glad you didn't have any trouble recognising me," said Mara. "The photo my publishers have been using is awful."

"No, it's perfect. You look just like that old movie star. What's her name? She was in the *Scream* films."

"Courteney Cox?"

"No! The other one."

"Neve Campbell?"

"Neve Campbell! That's it!"

"Nobody ever told me that before!"

"Honestly, it's a striking resemblance."

Mara liked this woman, whose manner was friendly and open. Despite being products of vastly different cultures, the fact that they were both female members of patriarchal societies meant they shared an understanding of victimization which enabled them to connect with each other in a way Mara strongly suspected she could never experience with any man. "How are you finding London?" she asked.

"It's pretty strange. It reminds me of Saudi Arabia before the revolution."

"I can imagine. I find it stranger all the time."

"I knew I'd have to wear a uniform," said Catherine, contemptuously tugging at her skirt, "but I didn't realise they wouldn't let me pass through customs until I'd bought one and changed into it."

"You can sell it back to the shop for half what you paid when you leave."

"I'm actually planning to take the Eurostar to Paris tomorrow, then fly home from there."

"I guess you can sell it inside the Eurostar terminal."

"My expense account will cover the cost, so maybe I'll keep it as a souvenir. Anyway, what with that and the flight being delayed, I was running late, so I came straight here instead of checking into a hotel first. That's why I'm dragging this suitcase around."

Mara had a spur-of-the-moment idea. "I live a few minutes away from the Eurostar. How about staying overnight at my place?"

"That would be fantastic! You're sure it's no bother?"

"I'd love the company, and we can do the interview more easily there."

As they left the bar, Catherine confessed to having specifically requested this assignment because she admired the Melissa Valance series. Since her readers were located in other countries, Mara rarely heard compliments about her work, and she listened contentedly as Catherine described how prominently the novels were displayed in American bookstores with well-stocked crime sections. Approaching a rank of taxis, Mara steered Catherine past the cars with 'Men Only' signs in their windows, and eventually found one that would take them where they were going.

Mara drew Catherine's attention to locations of historical interest during the short journey, pointing out the obvious contrast between those well-maintained buildings on Caledonian Road's right-hand side, where she lived, and the crumbling council estates on its left. The taxi soon came to a halt outside Mara's apartment, and Catherine paid for the ride by pressing her thumb onto the driver's scanner. As they climbed out, Mara and Catherine noticed a couple marching down the street, arguing loudly. Mara heard the man say, "Knock it off," and the woman reply, "You fucking knock it off." Having lost interest in this Socratic discourse, Mara was watching the driver remove Catherine's suitcase from the taxi's boot, and didn't observe what happened next: she just heard a thud and a scream. Turning around, she saw the woman on her knees, clutching her stomach, and the man standing over her with his fist clenched. The woman's mouth was opening and closing, as if she couldn't decide whether to express anger or plead for mercy. Catherine, clearly shocked, had retreated a few steps. Oblivious to the fact he had an audience, the man used one hand to grab hold of his partner's jacket, and the other to punch her in the face. There was a sickening crack, and Mara knew the woman's nose had been broken. Catherine gasped and backed towards the taxi.

Finally realising he was being watched, the man looked threateningly at Mara, then at Catherine, who cried "No, please!" and raised her arms defensively. The man shook his head in contempt and sauntered away without a backward glance as his victim climbed to her feet, blood running down the lower half of her face.

Mara was about to invite her inside, but before she had a chance to say anything, the woman shouted "Wait!" and ran after the man. Once she caught up with him, they walked along side by side. As far as Mara could tell, neither of them said another word.

Mara felt shaken by the incident, but Catherine was terrified: she leaned against the taxi, covering her mouth as if she feared the man might come back and assault her. Mara put a hand on Catherine's shoulder and said, "It's okay. He's gone. My place is over here." Catherine allowed herself to be led away.

Satisfied the show was over, the driver mumbled, "Bloody foreigners," climbed into his vehicle and drove off. Mara found this remark curious, since there was nothing about the couple to suggest they were foreign. Perhaps he was referring to Catherine. Or perhaps 'bloody foreigners' was a general term of abuse. She'd never understand London's taxi drivers!

As Mara pressed the thumbprint entry scanner outside her apartment, she noticed Catherine shaking like a leaf. Opening her front door, she guided Catherine down the hallway towards the guest bedroom, then ran into the living room and poured a glass of whiskey. When she returned, Catherine was sitting on the bed, taking a series of deep breaths. "I'm sorry for reacting like this," she gasped. "I've lived in New York all my life, but I've never seen anything like that."

Mara handed Catherine the glass and gently rubbed her back. "That kind of thing doesn't happen very often here, but I can't say it's the first time a woman has been beaten up on my doorstep."

"Shouldn't we call the police?" asked Catherine, drinking the whiskey in one gulp.

"They were probably married. There's no law against a man beating his wife. Legally, he can do pretty much anything short of killing her."

Catherine looked horrified. "What kind of country is this?"

"A very fucked up one," said Mara sadly as she walked into the hall and retrieved Catherine's suitcase. Catherine jumped up and took it out of her hands.

"What am I doing? I'm letting you fetch and carry for me like a servant! I'm so sorry I overreacted. I'm... I'm..."

"You're human. You're not used to violence. You react like a human being when confronted with it. Most of us don't. We sit back and watch as our humanity is eaten away bit by bit, holding on to whatever shreds we can."

"You seem to have held on to quite a bit of yours," remarked Catherine affectionately, adding, "This is a beautiful room," as she deposited her suitcase on the bed.

"It used to be my parents' bedroom," said Mara, distracted by a memory. "Anyway, would you like another whiskey, or could I make you a coffee, or something else?"

"No, really, I'm fine now. We can start the interview whenever you're ready."

"Let me get changed and I'll meet you in the living room."

As she approached her own bedroom, pausing by the front door to pick up some mail, Mara was haunted by the image of her mother's face, which she'd momentarily seen reflected in Catherine's. The resemblance was not physical, but rooted in a shared vulnerability. And Mara knew full well such delicate sensibilities could not survive the tide of brutality sweeping the country. Had Catherine lived in England, she would surely have succumbed as completely as Mara's parents. Mara was happy to think of Catherine sleeping in their room, and even happier to think of her leaving the next day. After changing back into the clothes she'd worn earlier, she checked her post. Aside from several pieces of junk, there was a literary quarterly she subscribed to, and a letter from the state religious authorities pointing out that her monthly church visit should take place within the next five days. It helpfully reminded her of the penalties for non-attendance, and expressed the wish that God would bless her.

Mara found Catherine standing in the living room, inspecting her bookshelves. She was amused to see that the journalist had also put on a pair of jeans and a T-shirt. "I didn't think anyone except me still read Joan Didion," said Catherine, looking up from the shelf she'd been examining.

"I guess we have a lot in common," responded Mara with a smile as she took a seat. "We even dress identically when we're not obliged to."

Catherine laughed and sat next to Mara. "I prefer this uniform."

Mara nodded. "I hate having to wear skirts. That's one of the reasons I don't go out much these days. I was home-schooled, so I could wear whatever I wanted, and I've always preferred masculine clothes. But my preferences no longer count for anything. There's a Japanese saying: *Deru kui wa utareru*. In English, it would be, 'The nail that sticks out gets hammered down'. That's me! I'm the kind of non-conformist our government had in mind when they passed the Compulsory Female Uniform Act."

"I can't understand why they found it necessary, though. It seems such an elaborate way of making some obscure point about gender roles."

"You have to remember that the men who run this country are products of the malinist movement. They believe gender roles are absolute, and should be enforced by law. Their definition of reality doesn't correspond with mine, but they have the power to impose that definition on me. It's all about control. Make a woman wear a skirt when she'd rather wear trousers, and you're forcing her to set aside her views concerning gender-appropriate behaviour and act in accordance with yours. Once you've established that kind of control, you can more easily take things to the next level. Look at the history of the Holocaust. If the Nazis had announced that they planned to wipe out Europe's Jewish population, there would have been an outcry, probably even armed resistance. So they started by disseminating antisemitic propaganda and forcing Jews to wear yellow stars, then banned them from working for newspapers, then from marrying or having sex with non-Jews, then from professional jobs, then from owning businesses, then from going to state schools, then from cinemas, then from all public places. After that, Jews were rounded up and sent to live in ghettos, where many died of starvation. It was only a short step from the ghetto to Auschwitz and Treblinka. If the Jews were willing to tolerate one thing, it was less difficult for them to tolerate the next, then the next. And that's essentially what's happening here. I'm not suggesting women will be exterminated; men still need us for breeding purposes if nothing else. But there's no way the British public would have accepted something like the Hunt if women hadn't already been categorised as lesser beings who can't vote, make reproductive decisions, or decide for themselves what they're going to wear. Once you've marginalised a group in this way, it's not so difficult to argue that its members should be hunted down like animals."

"Have you ever had to go on a Hunt?"

"No, but I've been eligible for the last four years, so I could be drafted any time."

"I can't imagine what it must be like living with that hanging over you. The main reason I'm leaving London so quickly is that I find the place scary."

"I suppose you can get used to almost anything. Apparently, some girls regard the Hunt as a rite of passage."

"Have any of your friends been conscripted?"

"No. Most of them are over thirty or male."

"You have male friends?"

"Yeah, there's still some good ones. My lover's eligible, but so far we've both been lucky."

"Your lover? So that means you're..."

Mara realised she'd been speaking too openly. "But none of this is for publication. Homosexuals are sent to prison here."

"Trust me, I won't repeat anything you just said, let alone include it in the interview. Speaking of which, shall we begin?"

"Yes, of course."

Catherine placed her mobile phone on a nearby table, pressing the record button as she did so.

"Let's start by talking about your background. Gorki's a Russian name isn't it?"

"Yes, but I'm so far removed from my Russian roots I couldn't tell you anything about them, though I love Russian literature."

"Maxim Gorky must have been one of your ancestors."

"He was, actually."

"You're kidding! I mean, I was kidding."

"Well, it's a very distant connection. His cousin was related to my grandfather in some way."

"So you have writing genes."

"The only thing my work has in common with his is its autobiographical basis."

"Does that mean you used to be a private detective?" "Oh, no. But Melissa Valance is basically me working as a private detective. Of course, she's a lot braver than me."

"How did you come to write the books?"

"It started soon after my parents died. They left me this place and some money, so I didn't have to worry about making a living. And I had plenty of time to read. Reading and watching films were the only things I really liked doing. But it frustrated me that I could never find any novels which dealt with life in Britain today. There were some, but they all felt divorced from reality. So I had the idea of creating a female British private detective, and setting her against a recognisable background. I started *Kill Me Goodnight* a few days after I turned twenty, and the first publisher my manuscript was submitted to accepted it right away. But the censor rejected it, so my agent suggested sending the book to America, and it took off straight away. I'm not entirely sure why. I guess Americans like getting a glimpse into what goes on in the U.K.. I wrote *Kill and Tell* the following year, and again the censor rejected it. I accepted that the books weren't going to be published here, which freed me up to start discussing things I felt passionately about. So the third book, *A Kill to Build a Dream On*, dealt with illegal abortion, something I'd never have attempted if I'd been hoping for British publication."

"Are you writing a new novel?"

"Absolutely. It's called *French Kill*, and it has Melissa investigating a murder that took place in Paris, even though she can't visit France to view the crime scene. Obviously, this book is going to focus on the law against women leaving the country."

"Your work has dealt with many of Britain's anti-female laws, but although you've touched briefly on the Hunt a few times, you've never tackled it directly."

"That's because people who haven't taken part in the Hunt only know vague things about what goes on, what Hunters do to women once they've caught them. I've heard rumours, of course, but...anyway, I couldn't describe a Hunt without experiencing one first-hand. Which I hope never happens."

"How about the scene in *A Kill Under the Mistletoe* where Melissa is flogged?"

"That happened to me, exactly the way it happened to Melissa, though my crime was being out of uniform. I needed some things from the local shop one winter evening, and since the temperature was close to zero, I decided to keep my jeans on. I'd gotten away with doing this several times before, and thought I'd be safe. But a police officer spotted me and scanned my thumbprint. A few days later, I received a registered letter ordering me to report to Camden Punishment Centre for ten strokes of the cane."

"That's outrageous!"

Mara shrugged. "Women can be caned just for wearing the wrong shade of tights, or skirts that cover any part of the leg below the knee. Going out in jeans was a stupid thing to do."

"Or a brave thing."

"If I'd really been brave, I'd have resisted their attempt to modify my behaviour. But the experience was so painful and humiliating I... I decided I wouldn't even try to leave my apartment again in... the wrong clothes. So you see, the... the beating had its desired effect, and turned me into a good girl who obeys the law. I have to be satisfied with expressing my frustrations on the page."

"Melissa's opinions obviously correspond closely to yours. I can see where her anger comes from. But are there more pleasant things about your life that you've used in the novels?"

"Oh, sure. You can see that this apartment, with its piles of books, is Melissa's apartment. Melissa's office is the room where I do my writing. And Melissa's assistant Wakako is based on my friend Yuke. Off the record, Yuke is my lover."

"I assume you made Melissa heterosexual to avoid arousing suspicions about your own sexuality."

"Exactly. Melissa is so obviously me that if I'd had her come out as gay, it would have started alarm bells ringing. I told you I wasn't brave. But Yuke is an important part of my life, so she had to be in the novels. The real Yuke is a film critic, and she was writing long before me. I wouldn't be able to work without her support. *Kill Me Goodnight* is dedicated to 'Y', and that's Yuke. But all the novels should be dedicated to her."

Mara decided to open a bottle of wine, and the conversation became more relaxed as they began discussing the similarities between Melissa Valance and other female private eyes, such as Sara Paretsky's V.I. Warshawski and Sue Grafton's Kinsey Millhone. When the interview ended, Catherine took some photos, and Mara ordered a takeaway curry. They spent the rest of the evening chatting about their very different lives.

The following morning, Mara walked Catherine to the Eurostar. Although Catherine was dressed identically to the other women they passed on the way, Mara noticed how the journalist's assertively unapologetic body language marked her out as the product of a society in which women believed themselves to have as much right as men to inhabit public spaces. While Catherine waited to board her train, she hugged Mara. "Thank you for being so considerate and putting me up last night. I can't wait to tell everyone I stayed in Melissa Valance's apartment! But don't worry. I'll be careful what else I say, even to people I trust. I know how rumours have a way of getting around. If there's anything I can do for you, please don't hesitate to ask."

"There is one thing. When you get back to New York, could you take some photos of the shelves in those stores you were telling me about? The ones where my books are on display. It's something I've never seen."

"It must be awful for an artist to be so cut off from her audience."

"It happened to Solzhenitsyn, Pasternak and Henry Miller, so I'm nothing special. At least there's no law against importing individual copies."

Catherine put her hand on Mara's shoulder. "Eventually, all this will change. Perhaps someday you'll be allowed to visit me in New York."

Mara smiled and said, "Yes, perhaps." But she sounded unconvinced.

The two women embraced once more, and Catherine ran to catch her train. Before disappearing behind the Eurostar gate, she turned and waved. Mara knew she would never see her again.

CHAPTER 2

As a child, Mara was protected from mid-twenty-first century Britain's worst excesses by her parents, a pair of radicals who raised their daughter to believe herself the equal of any man. Refusing to let her attend a state school, where she would inevitably be treated as a second-class citizen, they insisted on educating her themselves, ensuring she understood how the country had changed since the days of their youth. It was from her parents that Mara learned about Brexit, a chaotic process which enabled a fanatical right-wing government to pursue its reactionary agenda, beginning with the destruction of Britain's National Health Service. To Mara, the idea of healthcare being available to anyone who needed it, regardless of their financial position, was pure science-fiction, though she understood such things still happened in Europe. According to her parents, the NHS had once been part of everyday life, though by 2039, when it was officially abolished, it had long since been reduced to a pale shadow of its former self. Once the 'survival of the most privileged' principle had been established, the Conservatives felt free to run with it, drafting legislation which made life increasingly difficult for various minority groups. Over the next four years, state censorship was introduced for books, the press and the Internet - films having been subjected to such treatment since the 1980s - homosexuality outlawed, immigrants deported, and schools purged to eliminate Leftist teachers. The malinist movement, rooted in the theory that feminism was responsible for most of society's ills, didn't really get going until 2042, but once it started there was no stopping it. The Conservative assault on women's rights proved so savage it was difficult to believe the party had once been home to female MPs, even female Prime

Ministers. Politicians now adopted as their motto the Roman orator Cato's statement: "Give women freedom in one sphere and the floodgates of immorality will open in all the others." By 2043, the year Mara was born, women could no longer vote, seek public office, or be employed in any position a similarly qualified male had applied for. The compulsory uniform for adult females was introduced in 2044 - the state obviously considered men responsible enough to choose their own clothes, though transvestitism was illegal - and later that year, women were banned from driving, taking out mortgages, having abortions, and travelling abroad. Had the latter law not been passed, a significant number of women, Mara included, would eventually have travelled abroad and stayed there.

For although things seemed to have become as bad as possible, it turned out they could get worse. Much worse. On February 16th, 2059, three bombs went off in the Oxford Circus tube station during rush hour, resulting in the deaths of more than a hundred people. The following day, at least according to official reports, a militant feminist group calling itself Backlash claimed responsibility for the attack, and issued a manifesto which concluded: "We can no longer sit back and watch as our sisters are oppressed by the state. We demand equal rights, and if we cannot obtain them peacefully, we will take them by means of violence." None of the bombers were identified - they'd supposedly perished along with their victims - and Backlash was never heard from again. Indeed, aside from their strikingly banal and cliché-ridden manifesto, there was no concrete proof this mysterious terrorist group had ever existed. But public - which is to say male - fury was carefully stoked by the malinist press: "How Long Must We Live Under the Feminazi Jackboot?" screamed one tabloid headline.

Six days after the attack, Prime Minister Murdoch announced that he felt 'obliged' to take "unfortunate but necessary measures to remind women of their collective responsibility for an atrocity which has outraged every decent person." On May 3rd, the Hunt Act was passed, with the first Hunt scheduled for October. A stadium was constructed from what remained of an abandoned London district called Kilburn, and an announcement made that men interested in participating - and willing to pay for the privilege of doing so - should begin submitting their applications. Each Hunt involved ten men and ten women, and lasted seven days, a new event beginning two hours after the previous one ended. All females between the ages of twenty-one and thirty were declared eligible for the Hunt draft, and every week another ten were selected for compulsory participation. Mara's parents committed suicide by taking overdoses of sleeping pills in 2060, and though they hadn't left a note explaining their actions, Mara suspected the Hunt was to blame: the prospect of living in a society where such a thing could be contemplated, let alone carried out, would have been too much for the idealistic couple. By the time Mara turned twenty-one, the Hunt had been running nearly five years, and despite the nonchalant attitude she'd assumed for Catherine's benefit, thoughts of conscription caused her many sleepless nights.

The day after Catherine's departure was Friday, which meant that, as usual, Yuke would be coming over to spend the weekend. Yuke kept a change of clothes in Mara's apartment, and the only reason she hadn't moved in was that Mara worried about the kind of talk two theoretically unattached females living together might encourage. Yuke arrived at five p.m. carrying a pizza, changed out of her uniform, and settled down for a weekend of bad food, good movies and wonderful sex, interspersed with the occasional game of chess. When Mara read Tolstoy's *War and Peace*, she was struck by a passage describing Natasha's friendship with Princess Mary: "They were continually kissing and saying tender things to one other and spent most of their time together. When one went out the other became restless and hastened to rejoin her. Together they felt more in harmony with one another than either of them felt with herself when alone. A feeling stronger than friendship sprang up between them; an exclusive feeling of life being possible only in each other's presence." That was exactly how she felt about Yuke.

Yuke Morishita was the product of a Japanese family which had been living in England for several generations, and thus escaped the mass deportations of 2040. Yuke's parents wanted her to settle down with a nice Japanese boy, and would have had matching heart attacks if they'd even suspected she were sleeping with a Caucasian girl. So Yuke only saw her family at weddings and funerals - she could always tell which ceremony was which, because the funeral guests seemed more cheerful - a situation she felt extremely comfortable with.

Yuke had fallen under the spell of cinema while in her early teens, and used her natural brilliance to establish herself as a critic. She began writing professionally at the age of sixteen, and her articles exposing the flaws in diverse schools of advanced film theory earned her praise from the most respected names in the field. After her father referred to Yuke's career as a 'hobby' one time too many, she moved out of the family home in Amersham and into a small East Finchley apartment. Here she worked on what was to become her first book, an ambitious study of American cinema in the twentieth century. According to Yuke, classical Hollywood filmmakers challenged the status quo in ways that weren't appreciated at the time. "Look at Douglas Sirk," she'd demand enthusiastically. "He made commercial melodramas which were looked down on by mainstream critics but embraced by popular audiences. Yet they subjected the values of small-town America to devastating critiques. Senator McCarthy and HUAC were scared stiff of Leftists sneaking un-American messages into films, yet people like Sirk and Vincente Minnelli were doing this quite blatantly, without anyone even suspecting it." Mara loved to hear Yuke talk like this. It was one of these speeches that inspired her to create Melissa Valance, though her encounters with the censor suggested she lacked Sirk's talent for successful subversion. The Martin Beck novels of Maj Sjowall and Per Wahloo, which used thriller conventions to expose injustice in Swedish society, were another important influence. But her biggest inspiration was Yuke herself. Much as Mara feared being conscripted into the Hunt, she dreaded even more the day when she might have to look on helplessly as Yuke departed to spend a week being pursued and tortured by men who should have considered themselves lucky to live on the same planet as her.

The two women met in 2061, shortly after Mara turned eighteen, at a world cinema discussion group she attended regularly. This particular meeting was held inside a small bar located opposite the Renoir in Russell

Square, where they'd viewed that evening's film, Satyajit Ray's *Days and Nights in the Forest*. Yuke, who had just joined the group, was only seventeen at the time, and thus still permitted to wear her own clothes. As she eased herself into a chair next to this Japanese goddess in black Levi's and a 'Greta Garbo Lives' T-shirt, Mara felt painfully self-conscious, knowing how absurdly conformist she must look sitting there in her mandatory skirt and blouse. Yet in the course of talking about the film, Yuke took an obvious liking to her, and they started getting together regularly. Mara longed to let Yuke know how she really felt. Her fumbling experiences with men made it obvious there was little point in pursuing heterosexuality, but she lacked the courage to tell any woman, let alone the magnificent Yuke, that she desired her sexually. Her problem was solved in October when she attended Yuke's eighteenth birthday party at Cafe Koha, an underground bar which hosted private events. When Mara went to use the toilet, Yuke followed her, kissed her on the lips, then stood back and looked at her with trepidation, as if fearing Mara might run screaming from the room. Mara did not run or scream. She returned Yuke's kiss so passionately they came close to having sex right there. They somehow managed to contain themselves until the party ended and they'd taken a taxi back to Mara's apartment, where they spent the rest of the night exploring each other's bodies, finally falling asleep in a confused tangle of arms and legs as the light of dawn shone through the window.

When they awoke, Yuke confessed she'd never made love to a woman before, and apologised for her inexperience. Mara teased her for a few minutes, boasting of the parade of women who'd marched through her bed - so many she could no longer recall the precise number - before collapsing in a fit of laughter and admitting this was also her first time with a woman. Yuke had slept with men, and liked doing so well enough, but she'd never experienced this kind of passion with any of them. From that day, Mara and Yuke were a couple, and, had they not feared the consequences of exposure, would have been inseparable. Over the next six months, they decided to tell a few close acquaintances about their relationship, and a warmly protective support group grew up around them. Mara was especially pleased to discover how open-minded her male - and, so far as she knew, heterosexual - friends were. It made her suspect genuine potential for change existed, just waiting for somebody to tap it.

Mara and Yuke always spent Friday nights watching a film. Yuke was the expert in this department, but Mara's collection was impressive enough. As she ate the last slice of pizza, Yuke scanned the contents of Mara's DVD shelves, which she knew virtually by heart, and pulled out Max Ophuls' *Letter From an Unknown Woman*. They'd already watched this together three times, but Mara had no objection to doing so again. Afterwards, Yuke seductively removed her clothes and led Mara into the bedroom. When she could feel the slender weight of Yuke's naked body pressing down on her, Mara had everything she wanted, and her world was complete. If only it were possible to forget about the other world, the one outside her sanctuary. For the rest of the weekend, Mara and Yuke tried to do precisely that, spending Saturday ordering takeaway meals, watching DVDs, and making love.

They also cut each other's hair. Neither of them could be bothered with hairdressers, and Yuke's rough and ready trims were entirely adequate to Mara's needs. It was one more thing she didn't need to leave the apartment for. As Yuke snipped away with the scissors, Mara said, "Careful not to make it too short, honey." Mara would have preferred a buzz cut, but there were minimum hair lengths for women, just as there were maximum lengths for men, anything less than shoulder length being illegal. Mara was terrified of breaking the law - even such a minor offence would have earned her another visit to the punishment centre - but she suspected her terror was nothing compared to that felt by the men responsible for such absurd regulations, who surely lied awake nights desperately trying to convince themselves there was an unambiguous line dividing masculinity from femininity. If they ever acknowledged that the differences between men and women were primarily cosmetic - a matter of performance and training - the fragile foundations upon which their malinist ideology was constructed would come crashing down.

Mara had planned to stay in on Sunday, but Michael Cimino's *Heaven's Gate* was showing at the BFI, and Yuke, who had watched the film numerous times on disc, wanted to see it on the big screen. In the end, Mara was glad she'd let Yuke talk her into coming. Cimino's film spoke directly to the idea that, no matter how terrible things may seem, no matter how certain defeat may appear, there are always ideals and individuals worth fighting for. The appeal to communal values seemed especially powerful when the film was seen as they were seeing it now, with an appreciative cinema audience. Yuke had told Mara that the coda - in which Kris Kristofferson's character is alone on his yacht, surrounded by the emblems of wealth yet unable to forget what he has lost - always made her cry, and Mara deliberately looked at her while the scene was playing. Tears were indeed streaming down her face, and Mara realised she too was weeping, swept away by the power of great art. When the end credits finished rolling, Yuke enthusiastically led the applause, and the two women decided to visit the nearest female-friendly bar, which happened to be the one where Mara had met Catherine three days ago. They drank wine and discussed the film, wishing they could express their affections more directly. They'd almost certainly be safe doing so, surrounded as they were by fellow cinephiles, yet the risk didn't seem worth taking. Eventually, they walked towards Waterloo and caught the tube. Mara changed at Leicester Square, saying farewell to her lover in a casually friendly manner: displays of passion would really be inadvisable here. Yuke remained on the train until it reached East Finchley. As Mara arrived home, she reflected that it had been a perfect day. She had no way of knowing this would be the last good day for quite some time.

CHAPTER 3

On Monday, Mara awoke around eight and began her morning routine. She made breakfast, checked her email - Yuke had sent a message saying she couldn't wait for next Friday, to which Mara responded in kind - and eased herself into the day by lying on her bed and reading. She'd just started *The Aging Boy*, and wanted to know more about its author. According to Wikipedia, Julian Claman enjoyed a successful career as a television producer, but had only written two books, the other being something called *The Malediction*. Apparently, Larry McMurtry once described *The Aging Boy* as a great lost novel. Mara was grateful for the legal loophole which permitted books printed in the pre-censorship era to still be sold. *The Aging Boy* probably wouldn't qualify for a total ban if submitted to the state censor board, but cuts might be demanded, and even a truncated version would almost certainly receive an Unsuitable For Women rating. Mara had lost count of the times she'd tried purchasing a new novel in Foyles or Borders, only to have her attention drawn to the UFW certificate printed on the spine and back cover. She'd noticed the female staff in these stores were extremely apologetic - though they could get into as much trouble for selling her an 'inappropriate' book as she could for buying it - while the males tended to be contemptuous and even abusive. She now did her book shopping exclusively via second-hand stores and websites specialising in imported goods.

At nine-thirty, Mara changed into the uniform and headed towards her local church. Although British citizens could follow whatever religion they pleased, they were also required to spend at least two hours every month 'worshipping' in a Christian house of prayer. Mara usually chose Monday mornings, since they were quieter than other times. As she walked through the large doors of St. Pancras Parish Church, she placed her thumb on the scanner, which registered her attendance and collected an obligatory 'donation'. A nun standing by one of the pillars near the entrance gave her a friendly smile. Nuns were exempted from wearing the uniform, and much as Mara despised the ideology she represented, she found this woman striking in her long black habit. Something about her suggested she might be one of those rare professional Christians who actually followed Christ's teachings, and wished to make everyone feel welcome. By contrast, the priest who conducted Monday morning services seemed to have modelled himself on the God of the Old Testament. He had a long white beard, and addressed his flock in a booming voice. As Mara took a seat in the back row, he was declaiming a passage from Deuteronomy. A Bible lay open on the stand before him, but this section was one of his favourites - Mara had heard him recite it half-a-dozen times - and at no point did he refer to the text. "If the charge is true and no proof of the young woman's virginity can be found," he roared, staring at his captive audience as he did so, "she shall be brought to the door of her father's house and there the men of her town shall stone her to death. She has done an outrageous thing in Israel by being promiscuous while still in her father's house. You must purge the evil from among you. If a man is found sleeping with another man's wife, both the man who slept with her and the woman must die. You must purge the evil from Israel. If a man happens to meet in a town a virgin pledged to be married and he sleeps with her, you shall take both of them to the gate of that town and stone them to death—the young woman because she was in a town and did not scream for help, and the man because he violated another man's wife. You must purge the evil from among you."

If Mara hadn't already been a militant atheist, these mandatory church visits would have turned her into one. She sat in the back row, listening to the priest drone on, glancing at her watch every few minutes. She'd have brought a book, but reading secular texts here was a criminal offence. She noticed a pair of orthodox Jewish men sitting a few rows in front of her, looking uncomfortable and out of place. Eventually, the priest closed his Bible without so much as looking at it, cleared his throat, and delivered the day's sermon. "Many years ago," he began, "there lived a woman who thought of nothing but the joys of this world. She drank to excess, gorged herself on food, and copulated frequently, even with those of her own sex. Worse, she loudly proclaimed her defiance of God, denying His very existence. When death came to her, as it must to all of us, she was cast directly into Hell. There, she was hung naked in flames, her tongue removed with pincers, her eyes gouged out, her ears cut off, the flesh torn from her body, a hot poker inserted into the place from which she had derived such pleasure during her lifetime of sin. When this process had been completed, her body instantly regenerated, and the torture started anew, as it would continue to do forever. But still she defied God. She now admitted His existence, but declared this existence to be an abomination. Was it not God who had sentenced her to an eternity of suffering? God, she decided, was an immensely powerful sadist from whom there could be no escape. And for the first time, she knew the fear of God. She feared not the unending torments to which she was subjected, but rather that even in this place, where sinners were cast out of God's sight, He might reach down and pluck her out, like a rock buried in the ground, and thus bring her face to face with Him. Hell is so arranged that those condemned to a lower circle may never ascend to a higher, but there is nothing to prevent those on the higher circles descending to the lower. And so it was that this woman, acting on her demented beliefs, made a deliberate choice to sink further into the Pit. As she passed from one circle to the next, her agony increased, but the pain bothered her less than the idea that she was being pursued by God. Finally, she came to rest in the last of the nine circles, in the middle of which Satan himself squatted like a toad. Here, in addition to everything she had previously endured, cackling demons forced her to consume her own intestines, then her limbs, then the rest of her body. In the final seconds before regeneration occurred, her mouth turned inside out and consumed itself. But although she had now sunk as far as possible, the woman's greatest fear was that she had not sunk far enough, could never sink far enough. Even in the deepest pit of Hell, she was still not safe from God."

Mara wasn't sure whether to be more alarmed by the content of this vile lecture, or the priest's conduct while delivering it, for although she'd positioned herself at the rear of the church, she had no trouble seeing that he was vigorously masturbating under his cassock. Finally seeming to remember where he was, the man staggered out of his pulpit and disappeared through a door located behind the altar while the choir broke into *He Who Would Valiant Be*. As the congregation rose to its feet and made a desultory attempt to join in with the singing, Mara noticed two hours had passed since her arrival. She walked back to the entrance and once more placed her thumb on the scanner, confirming she'd stayed the required length of time. For some reason, the sermon echoed in her head. She didn't believe in Hell or Heaven, but try as she might, she couldn't shake the feeling that this dreadful tale contained an element of prophecy.

After changing into jeans and an old but extremely comfortable jumper, Mara settled down in her office chair and resumed work on *French Kill*. She decided to put the masturbating priest into the book, hoping her American readers wouldn't find him far-fetched. She wrote for an hour with an ease that only came when she was completely focused, and felt mildly annoyed when her doorbell rang. She briefly considered ignoring it, determined to at least finish the current sentence, but a second ring suggested her caller was growing impatient. As she strode into the hall, her face displayed a 'this better be good' expression. The bell rang a third time just before she yanked the door open and discovered a postman standing outside. Not the one who usually brought her mail, but rather an unfamiliar and strikingly dishevelled individual who, judging by the smell, hadn't washed in months. Mumbling something which sounded like "Banooseferoo," he held out a scanner.

"Excuse me?" said Mara.

"Special delivery!" said the man emphatically. Mara pressed her thumb onto the screen, and was handed a small package. The postman chuckled as she took it. "Banooseferoo," he mumbled again.

Mara looked at him in bewilderment. "I don't understand."

The man chuckled once more, sniffed loudly, and said, "Bad...news...for...you."

Mara watched as he strolled off down the street, wagging an admonishing finger in her direction while chanting, "Banooseferoo! Banooseferoo!" Disturbed by this bizarre behaviour, she shut the door and carried the package into her living room. Unsealing the flap, she noticed an official stamp just above the address. The stamp had been smudged, but the words 'Selective Service Board' were still visible. Mara felt her knees buckle, and heard herself say, "Oh no," as she dropped into the nearest chair. Hands trembling, she turned the package upside down. A pamphlet, a railcard, and a letter fell onto the floor. Her whole body shook as she picked up the letter, unfolded it, and began to read.

"To Mara Gorki.

Greetings.

You are hereby ordered to report for induction into the Hunt commencing Friday March 23rd and ending Friday March 30th.

Please find enclosed a pamphlet containing information about the role you will be expected to play in the Hunt, and a railcard which can be used on any branch of the U.K. overland rail and London underground on the days of your arrival and departure.

The Hunt Stadium is located opposite Hunt tube station (formerly Kilburn station) on the Jubilee Line. You are required to check in at reception no earlier than two-thirty p.m. and no later than three p.m. on the 23rd. Failure to do so will result in a warrant being issued for your arrest. If you believe you may be exempt from the Hunt on health grounds, it is your responsibility to obtain a medical certificate and deliver it to Hunt Administration no later than March 21st.

You must wear full uniform, including a jacket. Apart from the uniform, no personal belongings may be taken beyond the reception area. Belongings should be deposited with the receptionist when you arrive and collected as you depart.

David Wainwright
Head of Hunt Administration."

Mara felt sick to her stomach as she read this. Just a few minutes ago, everything had been fine. Now, the bottom had fallen out of her world. Today was the 12th. That meant she only had until the end of next week. She looked at the pamphlet: the words 'A Female Participant's Guide to the Hunt' appeared in large type on the front cover. She knew she'd have to read it eventually, and decided to get the unpleasant task over with.

"You are reading this pamphlet because you have been chosen by the Selective Service Board to participate in a forthcoming Hunt.

The Hunt was created in 2059 as a response to the February 16th bombing, a terrorist attack, perpetrated by a militant feminist group, which so appalled the people of Great Britain that drastic measures became necessary to make the country's female population realise such atrocities were not acceptable. You were almost certainly not directly connected with this attack, but it was carried out in the name of your gender, and you must accept the collectively imposed penalty. The Hunt is that penalty.

The Hunt Stadium, the bulk of which consists of the Hunt Arena, is located within the derelict London district of Kilburn. A wall was erected to seal off the stadium, an administration annex built, and a block containing ten Hunters' apartments constructed in the middle of the arena. Vending machines containing food and drink are located at irregular intervals throughout the arena. Apart from this, the area remains exactly the same as when as it was abandoned in the 2040s, and consists of several streets full of disused buildings.

Each Hunt involves ten male Hunters who have paid for the right to participate, and ten women between the ages of twenty-one and thirty, chosen by a process of random selection. Each Hunter has been assigned an apartment in the specially constructed block.

Once you arrive at the Hunt stadium, you will be taken to a meeting area in which you will spend thirty minutes being viewed by the Hunters, who may also engage you in conversation. After this, you will enter the arena. One hour later, the Hunters will be permitted to enter the arena and begin searching for you.

You may attempt to conceal yourself in any part of the arena, and take whatever evasive action you feel is necessary to avoid capture. However, assaults on Hunters are not permitted. Food and drink can be obtained from the vending machines, which are thumbprint operated. You may only take one food item and one drink item within a single six-hour period. The end of the Hunt will be signalled by a ten-second alarm, repeated at thirty-second intervals for a period of five minutes. If you have remained free for all seven days, you may proceed to the exit when you hear this alarm.

If you are captured by a Hunter, you will be taken back to his apartment in the middle of the arena. Each apartment contains a fully equipped playroom, and it is here that the Hunter will subject you to a variety of practices designed to cause pain and humiliation for as many days as remain in the Hunt.

The practices you may be required to endure are as follows:
- Striking of the buttocks, thighs, breasts, palms or soles with hand, cane, whip, paddle or strap.
- Striking of the arms, back or stomach with whip or strap.
- Non-consensual vaginal or anal intercourse. Condoms must be used at all times.
- Piercing of nipples or genitals with one-inch sterile needles. To avoid infection, each needle may only be used once.
- Shocks delivered via electrodes attached to any part of the body below the neck. Electrical devices in the playroom limit frequency and voltage to ensure safety. No shocks may be administered until consent has been given by a doctor.
- Insertion of no more than three fingers, or of devices intended for such a purpose, into vagina or anus.
- Clamps attached to nipples or genitals.
- Suspension by rope.
- Confinement in a cage designed to maintain a stress position for a period not exceeding eight hours.
- Straddling a wooden horse for a period not exceeding eight hours.

None of the following are permitted:
- Striking the face or head.
- Punches to any part of the body.
- Activities which threaten to cut off air supply, including strangulation, immersion in water and suspension by the neck.
- Activities which are likely to result in permanent injury or disfigurement (beyond light scarring), or are potentially life-threatening.
- Branding.
- Activities involving knives, scalpels or other sharp objects.
- Activities involving excrement or urine.
- Activities involving animals.

Once you have been captured, you will be examined by a doctor every twelve hours. Any complaints you may have concerning mistreatment must be made to this doctor at the first available opportunity. It is the Hunter's responsibility to feed you during your period of captivity. Hunters will be required to meet the costs of medical expenses resulting from their activities. Any Hunter whose behaviour results in the death of a captive will be prosecuted to the fullest extent of the law.

As soon as the alarm signalling the end of the Hunt has sounded, the Hunter must escort you to the arena exit. You will then be free to leave."

Putting down the pamphlet, Mara became aware of a warm feeling between her legs, and realised she'd lost control of her bladder. She ran to the bathroom, threw up in the toilet, and sat there with her head slumped over the bowl, trying to process the information she'd just received. She'd known the Hunt involved acts of sexual sadism, but had no idea such extremes were permitted. It resembled that demented priest's vision of Hell. She couldn't stop thinking about how the place where these things were done was called a 'playroom'. It was as if these men, these 'Hunters', were children playing with living toys. Using all her strength, she stood up, removed her wet clothes, and walked towards the kitchen. After throwing her jeans and underwear into the washing machine, she returned to the bathroom and took a shower. The hot water proved momentarily calming, and helped her to think clearly. Simply in order to maintain her sanity and get through the next few days, she needed to take a proactive approach. The first thing to do was consult a doctor and see if she could obtain an exemption. Stepping out of the shower, she dried herself and put on a bathrobe. Deciding to use the phone in her office - the thought of entering the living room and seeing that horrendous pamphlet again was intolerable - she called Soho Medical Centre and made an appointment for the following day, then slumped in her work chair, wondering what to do next. It would obviously be necessary to inform Yuke. She dreaded doing this, and her initial impulse was to put it off as long as possible. But her lover had the right to know, and if their positions were reversed, Mara would expect Yuke to share the news immediately. She couldn't cope with a phone conversation, though. Closing the text file she'd been working on before the doorbell rang, she accessed her email account and typed the following message:

"To: YukeMorishita2043@aol.com
From: Mara.Gorki@aol.com
Subject: Hunt
Dearest Yuke - This is one of the most difficult emails I've ever had to write. I just received a letter telling me I must take part in a Hunt. I will have to leave on the 23rd. I'm so scared."

Mara hit 'send' without giving herself a chance to think, then wondered if it had been a good idea to tell Yuke how scared she was. There was no need to upset her more than necessary, and it would be better to put on a brave face. She wrote another message:

"To: YukeMorishita2043@aol.com
From: Mara.Gorki@aol.com
Subject: Hunt 2
I'm seeing a doctor tomorrow. Maybe I can be exempted on health grounds."

Although Mara didn't really think she'd be exempted, this at least provided a faint glimmer of hope. But what should she do now? Resume work on her novel? The idea was laughable. She suddenly became aware of how tired she felt: it was as if the emotional exhaustion caused by her conscription had induced a state of physical exhaustion. She shuffled towards her bedroom, collapsed on the bed, and fell into a deep sleep filled with vague but disturbing dreams of pursuit and capture, from which she was awakened by the sound of a doorbell. Glancing at her bedside clock, she discovered she'd been asleep for almost three hours. Racing towards the front door, she yanked it open and found Yuke standing there with a look of distress on her face. Yuke embraced Mara without saying a word. Mara had managed not to cry so far, but with her face buried in Yuke's shoulder, the floodgates opened, and she sobbed uncontrollably while Yuke stroked her hair. Mara felt the desire to make love...no, not to make love, to fuck, mindlessly, to lose herself in physical sensation. She pulled Yuke into the bedroom. Yuke didn't have to be told what Mara needed and why she needed it. They spent the next two hours using their intimacy as a defence against the encroaching darkness, stopping only when they were too exhausted to continue.

As they lay side by side on the bed, Yuke put her arm around Mara and asked if she wanted something to eat. Mara noticed it was already seven o'clock. The whole day had passed in a haze, and she hadn't eaten since breakfast. They decided to send for a pizza, and Yuke walked out naked to the living room to place the order. Mara heard her talking on the phone, then waited for her to return. Several minutes passed, and Mara began to wonder if Yuke was okay. Tiptoeing into the room, she found Yuke sitting on the sofa reading the Hunt pamphlet, tears pouring down her face. As she heard Mara enter, Yuke looked at her with fierce determination and said, "We have to get you out of the country, or at least find a place for you to hide. We can't let them do these things."

Mara sat down next to Yuke and put an arm around her. "Honey, you know it's impossible. There's no way to leave the country, and if I tried to hide, they'd find me eventually. Then it would be even worse."

"But maybe...we could find someone at Dover who has a boat and..."

Mara kissed her on the cheek. "It wouldn't do any good, sweetie. Let me see the doctor tomorrow. If that doesn't work...well, it's only one week out of my life, and then I can put the whole thing behind me."

They sat there silently, waiting for the food to arrive. It wasn't until Mara heard the doorbell that she realised they were both naked; she hurriedly pulled on her bathrobe before opening the door and paying the deliveryman. After eating the food, Mara suggested they watch something depressing that would put her own problems in perspective, and eventually decided on Michael Haneke's *The Seventh Continent*, in which members of a family meticulously destroy all their possessions prior to committing suicide. The film made Mara recall her own parents' suicide, which also seemed to have been a protest against an intolerable situation. Would it have been better if they'd taken her with them? On the whole, she thought not. Despite the horrors awaiting her, she still loved life, and believed it worth fighting for. She felt strangely calm. She'd absorbed the bad news, and now experienced a sense almost of relief that the letter she'd been dreading for years had finally arrived. Despite having already slept for several hours, she was pleasantly tired. In bed, Yuke held her all night, and her presence kept away bad dreams.

CHAPTER 4

This, at least, was how it initially appeared to Mara. But just before dawn, she felt Yuke's grip tighten, and heard her moaning. That was when she realised Yuke had not kept away bad dreams, but rather absorbed them. Mara's first encounter with this mysterious talent occurred the night before her punishment centre appointment. Yuke had lain alongside her then as well, enabling her to enjoy a deep and dreamless sleep. When Mara had awoke, she'd seen that Yuke was covered in sweat, her head moving rapidly from side to side as she fought off some hallucinated torment.

Now the same thing seemed to be happening again. As Mara eased herself out of Yuke's arms and stroked her forehead, she heard her mumbling, "Please, don't. I beg you. I can't take it," then a few words in Japanese, and finally something which sounded like, "I can't move. All I can do is watch." Mara thought of Yuke as a dreamcatcher, but in a sense the process worked both ways.

Three years ago, Yuke had been groped in the street by a drunken police officer. She'd endured the assault for as long as possible, but when the man undid her blouse, pulled up her bra, and began caressing her breasts, she spat in his face. She was immediately arrested, and ended up being prosecuted for assault. The officer claimed he'd been sober and conducting a random search, and since a policeman's word counted for a lot more than that of a mere female, the trial was a perfunctory affair which lasted only ten minutes. It concluded with the Judge sentencing Yuke to have the little finger on her left hand removed. Yuke was required to pay for the operation, which would be carried out without anaesthetic: it cost more than she earned in six months. She had medical insurance, but judicial amputations weren't covered by her policy, since her healthcare provider classified them as 'unnecessary surgery'. Mara insisted on selling some stocks she'd inherited to help raise the money. Other than that, there didn't seem to be anything she could do to alleviate Yuke's distress.

When the day of the operation arrived, Mara accompanied Yuke to the hospital, but had to watch helplessly as her lover was taken into the operating theatre. While she sat in the waiting room, Mara noticed that the little finger on her left hand had begun to ache. She put this down to sympathy pains, and forget all about it when Yuke reappeared two hours later, her face streaked with tears and a large white bandage wrapped around her hand. Acting on the orders of the court, the surgeon had injected Yuke with a pain enhancer, as well as a drug designed to neutralise the effect of painkillers for twenty-four hours. She spent the rest of the day curled up in a ball on Mara's bed, eyes tightly closed, screaming in agony. In the evening, however, Mara's own hand started throbbing again. She looked at it, and was astonished to see that the little finger had swelled to twice its normal size. As Mara's discomfort increased, Yuke's sobs lessened. Towards midnight, Yuke opened her eyes and said, "It's so strange. My hand's gone completely numb." By this point, Mara was in such agony she could barely speak. Yuke rested peacefully for the rest of that night, while Mara lay there with her face buried in a pillow, trying to stifle her cries. The next morning, Mara's pain gradually decreased as Yuke's returned, but the injection wore off later that afternoon, and a powerful analgesic soon put an end to Yuke's torment. From that day, the two women knew their connection to be more powerful than any of the brutal masculine forces arrayed against them. The symbolism of the amputation was clear enough: Yuke had defied a representative of patriarchal law, and been subjected to an act of castration. But every time Mara looked at the stump on Yuke's hand, she thought less of powerlessness than of the specifically female strength represented by their bond.

And now, this bond was making its presence known once more. Mara shook Yuke gently, trying to ease her out of the nightmare. Yuke awoke almost instantly, sitting up and gasping for air. It was not necessary for either of them to say a word about what had happened. They never talked directly about their shared talent, perhaps fearing that exposing this gift to the cold light of rational discussion would cause it to vanish.

While Yuke took a shower, Mara went to check her email. Her inbox contained seven new messages which seemed almost absurd in their ignorance of her changed circumstances. How could she concern herself with an amusing photograph, a link to an article on detective fiction - in which Melissa Valance was briefly mentioned - or a dinner invitation? Such things belonged to another person, another world. She tried convincing herself that there was still some hope of returning to that world, that the doctor might ride to her rescue, like a knight on a white charger. But she knew full well the chances of this happening were virtually nonexistent. She thought of the door-keeper in Kafka's *The Trial*, who tells the man attempting to bribe him, "I take this only to keep you from feeling that you have left something undone."

At twelve-thirty, Mara and Yuke changed into their uniforms and set out for the Soho Medical Centre. Soho was London's salvation district, its streets dotted with neon signs reading 'Licensed Church Downstairs' or 'Souls! Souls! Souls!', and anyone having non-religious business in the area was obliged to run a gauntlet of aggressive priests trying to drum up business. The Soho churches' main attraction was that their obligatory donation fees tended to be considerably lower than those charged by more mainstream institutions, but they were notoriously dangerous places in which women ran the risk of being raped, sometimes by the priest conducting the service. As Mara and Yuke ascended the medical centre's steps, they noticed an angry-looking man wearing a clerical collar standing in the doorway of the Christ club next door. "Step inside and be saved!" he shouted. "Two for the price of one!"

Mara's appointment was for one-thirty, but there were always delays, and she didn't end up seeing the doctor until almost two. She'd encountered few health problems in her life, and as a result had never previously met Dr. Rodman, the man who was theoretically her GP. He turned out to be a tall, friendly individual who asked her what the problem seemed to be in a tone of voice which suggested that whatever it was, he could make it go away with a flick of his prescription pad. Mara decided the straightforward approach would be best. "I've just been conscripted into the Hunt, and wondered if there was any way I could be exempted on medical grounds."

"And what do you think is wrong with you?"

Mara wasn't certain how to answer this. She could hardly point out that torture might be hazardous to her health. "I'm not really sure," she mumbled.

The doctor nodded understandingly. "Go behind the curtain, take your clothes off, put on a robe, and we'll have a look at you."

Mara did as she'd been told, and Dr. Rodman, with the assistance of a nurse, gave her a thorough examination, including a test for blood pressure. After the nurse had left and Mara was dressed again, the doctor asked her to sit down.

"Well, you're in perfect health. Normally, I'd say that was good news, but in your case I suppose it's a mixed blessing."

Mara shuddered as she heard this. She hadn't expected a different verdict, but this had been her one hope, and now that it was gone, the reality of the Hunt loomed over her more terrifyingly than ever.

"Couldn't there be a psychological reason for me to be exempted?" she asked desperately. "I'm so scared, I've seriously been contemplating suicide."

The doctor seemed to see this blatant lie for what it was. "I wish I could help you, but if I provided a medical exemption to every healthy young woman who didn't want to take part in the Hunt, then pretty soon nobody would be taking part in the Hunt. As far as I'm concerned, that would be an excellent thing, but the reality is I'd lose my job. Your ordeal will be closely supervised by a qualified doctor, and he'll make sure you don't suffer any permanent damage. Come see me when you get out and I'll ensure you receive whatever treatment is necessary. If you have to be hospitalised, list me as your doctor and I'll examine you there. And who knows, perhaps you'll manage to avoid capture."

"Have many of your patients been in the Hunt?"

"Certainly. I've received specialist training in post-Hunt trauma."

"Do you know of anyone who managed to avoid capture for all seven days?"

The doctor was unable to meet Mara's gaze. "I...I can't discuss the details of my patients' lives. You understand, I'm sure."

Mara thanked the doctor and departed.

Yuke looked up from her seat in the reception area as she saw Mara approaching. Mara shook her head and said, "Well, back to the drawing board," with as cheerful a tone as she could muster before walking over to the woman behind the counter and settling her bill. Yuke wished she could take Mara's hand to comfort her, but it was necessary for them to maintain their distance.

As they left the medical centre, Mara had to lean on Yuke for support. The last remaining barrier between herself and the Hunt had come crashing down. She stared at the pedestrians carrying on with their everyday activities, apparently oblivious to the fact that at any moment a chasm might open beneath their feet. Mara felt as if she'd been made privy to a terrible truth of which these people had no knowledge, like one of those H. P. Lovecraft characters who glimpses an infernal universe concealed behind the thin veneer of mundane reality, constantly threatening to break through and assert its dominance. The priests shouting at her as she staggered along the street now seemed almost demonic.

Mara needed to take some kind of action - anything that would help her cope with the next few days - and as soon as she arrived home, she asked if Yuke could think of any way to contact somebody who had participated in a Hunt, adding, "I'd like to get some practical advice."

Yuke brightened at this suggestion. She felt helpless, and being given a task provided her with a sense of purpose. "I'm sure my friends will be able to put me in touch with somebody."

They agreed that Yuke would return to East Finchley until Friday, giving Mara some space to come to terms with her situation and resume work. Mara was sorry to see Yuke go, but maintaining a calm facade for her benefit was becoming increasingly difficult. She turned on her computer and opened the *French Kill* file. The text broke off in the middle of the sentence she'd been composing when the postman arrived yesterday. How much had changed since then! But an interrupted sentence is easy to complete, and Mara was soon pounding away at the keyboard as if Melissa Valance's current case were her sole concern.

She worked for five hours, then made a snack and, though it was only seven o'clock, decided to spend what remained of the evening in bed. *The Aging Boy* was proving highly engrossing, and she read until well past midnight. The experience of being able to escape her troubles by writing and reading made Mara feel a connection with other writers, both living and dead. It gave her a much-needed sense of community, something that was always welcome, since it existed only in marginalised forms today. What kinship could she possibly feel with men who would enjoy torturing her?

As she unsuccessfully attempted to sleep, Mara began thinking about something that happened in 2051, when she was eight years old. A woman had stayed in the apartment for a week, sleeping on the living room sofa. But this was clearly no ordinary houseguest. Mara's parents usually made a point of introducing their daughter to their friends, and even including her in adult conversations, most of which went right over her head. But they deliberately kept her away from this visitor, whom they addressed in hushed tones behind closed doors. All they told Mara was that nobody must know about the woman. Mara only talked to her once, after waking in the middle of the night and getting up to use the toilet. Passing the living room, she noticed the door was open, and a light on. Looking inside, she saw the woman sitting up, writing in a notebook. The woman appeared to be around thirty, had bright red hair, and was strikingly thin and pale. She beckoned Mara to enter. Mara was nervous, but didn't want to appear rude, so she approached the sofa.

"You must be Mara," said the woman, putting down her notebook.

Mara nodded and asked, "What's your name?"

"Do you think names are important?"

"Not really. But it's important to have one."

"Quite so. You may call me whatever you wish. Rosa Luxemburg, perhaps, or Sophie Scholl."

"Rosa's a nice name."

"Then Rosa it shall be."

"Why are you staying here, Rosa?"

"Because I'm hiding."

"Why are you hiding?"

"Because men are trying to find me."

"But why are they trying to find you?"

"Because I'm hiding."

"So it's a kind of game."

"That's exactly correct. People often use theories to explain what is happening today. Political theories, sociological theories, financial theories, psychological theories, feminist theories, malinist theories. But the truth is as you say: it's a game. Shirts against skins. Men against women. Boys against girls. At the moment, we are playing hide and seek. The girls hide, and the boys, they seek."

"What will happen if the boys catch you?"

"They'll pinch my arms and make me cry. But these boys are expert pinchers, Mara, and if they pinch hard enough, I might tell them where the other girls are hiding. And that would be very bad. Do you understand?"

Mara had understood, probably for the first time in her life. The woman had gone on to say many things Mara could not comprehend then, and which she failed to recall now, but the image of a game played for genuine stakes was one she'd never forgotten. And since participation in the Hunt was inevitable, this childhood memory seemed the best way to make sense of her forthcoming ordeal. She would be required to play hide and seek. And if found, she would be pinched. Pinched hard.

CHAPTER 5

When Mara checked her email the following morning, she found a message from Yuke.

    From: YukeMorishita2043@aol.com
    To: Mara.Gorki@aol.com
    Subject: Claire
    Hi honey
    Are you feeling better today?
    I asked around, and have been told you should get
    in touch with a woman named Claire Richardson, who
    took part in a Hunt 18 months ago and would be
    willing to talk about it. I've never met her, but
    her boyfriend is a friend of mine, so she knows who
    I am and is expecting to hear from you. Her email
    is Claire.Richardson2039@yahoo.com.
    I love you so much. I'll always be there for you.
    xxxxxxxxxxxxxxx
    Y.

Mara sent a response thanking Yuke, and composed a carefully worded email to Claire.

    zFrom: Mara.Gorki@aol.com
    To: Claire.Richardson2039@yahoo.com
    Subject: The Hunt
    Dear Miss Richardson,

You don't know me, but I'm a friend of Yuke Morishita. I recently learned I will have to participate in a Hunt which begins next Friday. I would like to obtain as much information as possible about methods of avoiding capture. If you'd be willing to share information with me, whether by phone, by email, or in person, I'd greatly appreciate it.

Yours
Mara Gorki.

After hitting 'send', Mara, thinking it best to keep her mind as occupied as possible, resumed work on *French Kill*. The writing went well - it didn't flow as freely as usual, but was pretty good considering the circumstances - and she'd been working for almost two hours when her computer alerted her to the arrival of an email from Claire.

From: Claire.Richardson2039@yahoo.com
To: Mara.Gorki@aol.com
Subject: Re: The Hunt
Dear Miss Gorki,
My boyfriend told me I might be hearing from you. I am sorry to learn of your predicament. I was captured on the second day of my participation in the Hunt, and would be happy to talk to you about what happened prior to that. I think the information will be helpful. But I would prefer not to talk about what happened after I was taken captive. I'm cautious about what I say over the phone or by email, but please feel free to call on me any time. My address is:
27 Upper David Cameron Road
SW16
I will be home for the rest of today, and all of tomorrow.
Yours,
Claire Richardson.

Mara looked up the address. It was in Tooting, an area she'd never visited before. Deciding to set out immediately, she emailed Claire saying she'd be coming over, and changed into her uniform. Since the tube journey would take almost an hour, she slipped *The Aging Boy* into her jacket pocket.

The Northern Line platform at St. Pancras was surprisingly quiet for a weekday afternoon. The first train to arrive included Tooting Bec among its destinations. Mara was glad she wouldn't have to go through the tedious process of changing to another line. She grabbed a seat and began reading her book. There were only a few passengers, and when the train arrived at Elephant & Castle, Mara noticed she had the carriage entirely to herself. She relished the quiet atmosphere. But at the next stop, six young men strode through the doors, talking loudly among themselves. Instead of sitting down, they walked towards Mara and stood over her.

Mara shuddered. She had some idea of what was going to happen, having found herself in similar situations twice before. The first occurred four years ago. She'd been walking home when a group of teenagers had run up to her and started making suggestive remarks. Mara had tried to walk away, but they'd blocked her path. Repelled by their obscene comments, she'd made a crack about the average size of their penises, and the boys had responded by assaulting her. Physically, the attack was relatively mild - they'd slapped her face and the back of her head, poked her in the stomach and kicked her shins - but Mara had never felt so humiliated. She'd been afraid to leave her apartment for weeks afterwards.

The second incident took place on the tube last year. The age and behaviour of the aggressors was more or less the same, but that time Mara had tried flirting with them, insisting they were exactly her type, and promising to meet them later. Rather than falling for this act, the boys had pulled Mara out of her seat and thrown her onto the floor. Undeterred by the presence of other travellers, all trying to pretend nothing was happening, they'd started removing her clothes, and would almost certainly have raped her had the train not stopped at a station, allowing a crowd of late night revellers to enter.

Mara hadn't reported either incident to the police. What would have been the point? Now, it seemed, she was about to be attacked again. The boys surrounding Mara were standing there silently, staring at her. Mara kept her eyes on her book, hoping they'd go away if she didn't acknowledge them. After a minute or two, one of the boys waved his hand over the page she was attempting to read. This earned an appreciative chuckle from his followers. There always seemed to be a boy who functioned as ringleader in these groups, and from whom the others took their cue. Mara acted as if she hadn't noticed anything. This brought another chuckle from the boys. A few seconds later, the ringleader placed his hand on the book and pushed it down. "What's your name?" he asked. Mara remained silent, and tried to lift the book, but the boy pulled it out of her hands and glanced at the cover. "Oh, sorry," he said tauntingly. "I've lost your page. Do you remember what page you were on?" Mara still hadn't looked up. The boy clicked his fingers in front of her face and shouted, "Wakey! Wakey! I asked if you remembered what page you were on."

Mara could see that ignoring these thugs would only encourage them. She looked into the ringleader's face. He didn't seem any different from the last two boys who had attacked her. They could almost have been brothers. The same piggy eyes, the same slack jaws. "Look," she said as neutrally as possible. "I'm sitting here minding my own business. I'd appreciate it if you'd leave me alone."

The boy adopted an expression of mock outrage. "I was just trying to help you remember what page you were on. Tell me what was going on in the last paragraph you read."

"Please, just give me my book back," said Mara, holding out her hand as she did so.

The boy held the book above his head. "What do you need it for if you can't remember what page you were on?"

At that moment, the train pulled into a station, and its doors opened. Mara tried to stand up, saying, "This is my stop," but one of the boys who had previously remained in the background pushed her back into the seat.

The ringleader leaned down with an expression that was a hideous caricature of concern. "I'm sorry I lost your page. Now I want to repair the damage I've done. Tell me what the book's about. Maybe that'll help you remember where you were."

Mara prayed somebody would enter the carriage, but the doors swung shut again and the train resumed its journey. She looked up pleadingly, and asked, "Why are you doing this? What do you want of me?"

The ringleader pretended to be puzzled. "I already told you. I want to help you find your page." Mara knew nothing would deter these hooligans, so she might as well keep quiet and let them get on with it. The ringleader turned around to address his followers. "Obviously," he said, "we'll have to do this systematically." Opening the book, he chose a random page, ripped it out, and dangled it in front of Mara. "Was this the page?" Mara stared into space.

"Nah!" shouted one of the boys in the background. "That ain't it."

The ringleader crumpled up the page, dropped it onto the floor, and tore another from the book. "How about this one?" he asked, thrusting it into Mara's face. When she didn't respond, he again crumpled the page in his hand and tossed it over his shoulder. "This one?" he asked, repeating the process. "This one?" No response. "This one? This one?" By now, the boy was tearing entire sections from the book, ripping them apart, and throwing them into the air. Mara had been determined not to cry, but as page after page was held before her, she felt tears running down her cheeks. "Don't be sad," mocked the ringleader. "I'm sure we'll find the right page soon."

"Hey!" interjected one of the followers, tapping him on the shoulder. "I just thought of something. Even if we do find the page, it won't do her any good."

"Why not?" asked the ringleader, as if genuinely confused.

"Because you've torn up so much of the book, she wouldn't be able to finish it anyway."

The ringleader slapped his own head - the sound made Mara jump - and turned towards his victim with an expression of regret and disappointment. "Why didn't you point that out to me?" Mara wiped away her tears. These young sadists had what they wanted. They'd humiliated her, made her feel powerless, made her cry. Now perhaps they'd leave her alone. The ringleader gripped what was left of the book in both hands, pulled it in half, and deposited the remains in Mara's lap. "Do you have anything else to read?" he asked with another expression of mock sympathy. Mara shook her head, not looking him in the eyes. "Find her something," he shouted, and the other boys began running around the carriage in a parody of frenzied activity.

"Here!" announced one, picking up a newspaper that had been left on the floor.

He handed the paper to his leader, who put it in Mara's hands, saying, "There you are." Mara remained silent. The boy stooped until he was nose to nose with Mara. "What do you say?" he hissed.

Mara tried to avoid his gaze, but it was impossible. "Thank you," she whispered.

"You're welcome," said the ringleader, standing up. "But it was Dave who found the paper. He's the one you should thank. Come here, Dave." Dave approached Mara and occupied the position just vacated by his leader. "Well?" shouted the ringleader in the background.

"Thank you," whispered Mara again.

Dave smiled and asked, "Are you going to give me a thank you kiss?" Mara shook her head. The boy gripped her chin, said, "Don't be shy," and kissed her roughly on the lips. She felt like throwing up.

The train pulled into another station, and Mara was relieved to see people waiting on the platform. Noticing the same thing, the ringleader shouted, "This is our stop, lads." The gang followed him towards the doors and waited for them to open. As they left the train, they waved at Mara, and banged on the window behind her. Once the doors had closed again, Mara buried her head in her hands and sobbed. These boys had been determined to teach her a lesson, and they'd done so. This was how easily men, even young men, could dominate women. Reporting them would have done no good: the police were hardly likely to issue an all-points bulletin for a teenager who had torn up a book, which as far as they were concerned would have been all the incident amounted to. How could Mara explain that the gang's treatment of her amounted to rape, that they'd rendered her completely helpless, made her experience what it was like to be nothing, nobody. These were exactly the kind of individuals who, if they could afford it, would participate in the Hunt when they grew up. Mara felt she'd been given a preview of what was going to happen at the end of next week. She tried pulling herself together. She'd be in Tooting shortly, and had no intention of burdening Claire with her latest humiliation.

When the train arrived at Tooting Bec, Mara left the station and walked down Tooting High street. Tooting had once been home to many artists and writers, and until three years ago was among the few London suburbs with a Labour MP, but rising house prices had forced out most of the people who'd made it such an desirable place to live, and the area had undergone a process of gentrification, something made blatantly obvious by the 'men only' sign displayed in a pub window.

Claire's house turned out to be a ten-minute walk from the station. It was surprisingly big, but, at least from outside, seemed badly in need of repair. Mara rang the old-fashioned bell, and a few seconds later the door was opened by a woman wearing black trousers and a baggy jumper. "You must be Mara," she said with a faint smile. "I'm Claire." They shook hands, and Claire stood aside to let Mara enter. Claire couldn't have been much older than Mara, but she gave the impression of having been prematurely aged by some terrible trauma. The house was in much better condition than its exterior suggested, and Mara suspected that Claire shared her preference for the internal world. The walls were lined with remarkable paintings, all obviously by the same person, depicting grotesquely distorted androgynous figures. They reminded Mara of Francis Bacon's work, but there was something fiercely idealistic about the respect they showed for their tormented subjects. The paintings appeared to have been created by somebody willing and even determined to confront the worst life had to offer, yet retain a fundamental optimism. Mara suspected she knew who the artist was.

"Are these paintings by you, Miss Richardson?"

"Please, call me Claire. Would you like something to drink?"

Mara requested a glass of water. She couldn't help noticing that her question hadn't been answered. Maybe Claire had a reason for not wishing to discuss her work. She decided not to pursue the subject.

Mara was shown into the living room, which she was pleased to see contained several bookshelves; the presence of books always made her feel at home, as if they were the emblems of a secret society. Perhaps she should have brought one of her novels as a gift. Or would that have been egotistical? The two women sat in facing armchairs, and Claire broke the ice by saying, "I can't tell you how sorry I am you have to deal with this. It's a cliche to say I understand what you're going through, but I guess that's why you're here. Forget what I wrote in the email. If you need to hear about what that bastard did to me, I'll tell you everything."

"I don't want to make you dwell on that. I just need to know what happened when the men were chasing you."

"Well, you have an hour in the arena before the Hunters arrive. The big mistake we made was wasting that hour. We were ten terrified young women suddenly thrown into what looked like a war zone. Our instinct was to herd together for comfort and amble along the street as if we were on holiday. At some level, we simply hadn't let ourselves confront the reality of the situation. We thought that if we ignored it, it would ignore us. We didn't even use the vending machines, though we walked right past one. We were still within sight of the entrance when the Hunters came in. They obviously couldn't believe their luck when they saw all ten of us just standing there. They didn't know the arena any better than we did, but they were in the dominant position, and they just charged. As soon as we saw them coming, we at least had the sense to run in different directions, but it's difficult to run in those fucking skirts, and I think five of us were taken within seconds. The Hunters had these devices I assume were Tasers. Whatever they were, as soon as a woman was touched with one, she fell down. I only managed to get away because nobody was chasing me. You had several men running after the same woman, probably because she was the one nearest them. If it hadn't been for that, they'd have caught us all immediately. I ran around a corner and down an alleyway, hoping to throw them off. And it worked for a while. Then I saw this tall building which looked like it belonged on another planet. It seemed to have no connection with the surrounding rubble. It was the Hunters' apartment block. I was standing in front of it when a Hunter arrived carrying an unconscious woman. He had her slung over his shoulder, like a sack of potatoes. I was so scared I couldn't move. But the fucker just smiled at me and went into the building. I suppose he didn't need another victim. I felt like fainting, but I managed to run in the other direction. I eventually came to this old office building, and thought I'd try hiding in there for a while. There was a vending machine nearby, so I took a sandwich and a bottle of water, and climbed up the stairs to the fifth floor. There must have been fifteen floors, but the fifth seemed safe enough. I went into the first office I found. There was nothing inside it but old filing cabinets and a broken chair. The window was filthy, but it gave me the opportunity to see what was going on outside. That's the advantage of a dirty window; it's easier to see out than in. Every so often, I'd observe men walking along the street holding these machines with illuminated screens. They looked kind of like laptops. I think they were body heat detectors. But they were so small, they would only have been able to pick up somebody within the immediate area, and I was high enough to be out of range. Anyway, as it started to become dark, I noticed men wearing infra-red goggles. There's no electricity in the area, except in the Hunters' block, and no street lights, so at night the arena is pitch black. Whatever you do, don't move around in the dark; you'll be a sitting target. I somehow managed to sleep for a few hours. When I woke up just after dawn, I was desperate for a drink, but I'd already finished my water, and didn't dare go outside to use the vending machine. So I stayed by the window and stared at the street below. After a few hours, I spotted this one guy I hadn't seen since the Hunters viewed us in the meeting area. I remembered him because the creep shook my hand and said he looked forward to getting to know me. He was strolling along, calm as you please, scrutinising a handheld device. It wasn't one of those body heat detectors. Much smaller. But whatever it was, he seemed to be paying close attention to it. He walked right up to the building I was hiding in and went directly to the entrance. Didn't even glance at the other buildings. Then I heard him coming up the stairs. He didn't stop at any of the other floors, just walked straight up to the fifth. Of course, I was trapped. There was only one door to the office, and I had nowhere to run. When he came through the door, he didn't seem surprised to see me kneeling by the window. I don't know how, but he'd found some way of tracking me. He was wearing a backpack; as he walked towards me, he took it off, dropped it on the floor at my feet, opened it, and took out a Taser. He waved the Taser in my face and said, 'We can do this the hard way or we can do it the easy way'. I looked up at him and said, 'Easy way', in this pathetic voice. He put the Taser away and took a steel collar out of the backpack. He handed it to me, and told me to secure it around my neck. It fastened at the back, and once it was locked on

I couldn't remove it. He showed me this remote control he wore on his wrist, told me it was connected to the collar, and said that by pressing a button he could immobilise me, even if I was a mile away. He didn't demonstrate it then, but he did later, and he hadn't been bluffing. Then he commanded me to walk in front of him, and directed me to the Hunters' block. Once we were there…you can guess the rest."

Mara hardly knew what to say. "I want you to know how much I appreciate your sharing all this with me."

"If any of this helps you stay out of the clutches of those bastards for one extra minute, it'll have been more than worth it. Is there anything else you'd…like me to tell you?"

Mara shook her head. "You don't need to talk about what he did."

Claire turned away, staring blankly at her bookshelves. "He had me for six days," she said in a voice choked with emotion. "He did everything to me. Everything." Mara leaned over and embraced her. Claire regained her composure and looked Mara in the face. "And the truly terrible thing is that he did it because our government, which is supposed to represent the will of the people, passed a law saying he had the right to do it.' She gestured at her books. 'Have you read *Nineteen Eighty-Four*? Orwell almost had it right. He was very close. What he should have said was: If you want a vision of the future, imagine a man's boot stamping on a woman's face - forever."

CHAPTER 6

Mara spent Thursday working solidly on *French Kill*. It seemed like a good idea to finish the book before the Hunt, since she had no idea what condition she'd be in afterwards. Permanent injury was explicitly forbidden, but who could say what effect being tortured might have on her ability to create? It had only been a few days since Mara had insisted she couldn't write about the Hunt because she didn't have enough first-hand information. That problem was about to be solved! It seemed inevitable that, if she were still capable of writing at all, her next novel would involve Melissa Valance being drafted into the Hunt. Thinking professionally, Mara started to wonder how she could introduce the investigation of a crime into this scenario. But it was rapidly becoming clear to her that the real crimes investigated by Melissa were those committed within the boundaries of the law by the state and its representatives. In *A Kill to Build a Dream On*, a man hires Melissa to track down the individual who performed an illegal abortion on his wife, resulting in her death. When she locates the abortionist, Melissa determines that the woman is carrying out terminations in a safe and professional manner. Melissa eventually finds out that the wife died because of a beating her husband gave her after learning of the abortion. She reports this crime to the police, but the Director of Public Prosecutions refuses to press charges, insisting an all-male jury - the only kind permitted - would never find a husband who has beaten his wife guilty of manslaughter, especially under these circumstances. They'd be more likely to give him a medal. Instead, the abortionist is arrested and sentenced to life imprisonment.

French Kill was proceeding along similar lines. Melissa investigates the murder of a British woman who moved to Paris a few days before the law forbidding women from leaving the U.K. came into force. Melissa discovers that the woman had been writing articles for European newspapers exposing the injustices of British society, and was probably murdered by a hitman under contract to somebody connected with Britain's Prime Minister. Melissa learns that she'd been hired by a government representative who was under pressure to be seen doing something about the murder, and who asked her to investigate because he believed a private detective who couldn't travel to France would be unable to solve the crime. Like so many shady characters in these books, he hadn't reckoned on Melissa's resourcefulness.

Mara knew she was courting danger with these novels, but there was no law against writing for foreign publication. At least not yet. She worked until late at night, managing to complete a first draft before going to bed. She could start the final edit on Monday, and hopefully have it ready for her publisher in a few days. But work would have to be suspended over the weekend, which she planned to spend with Yuke. She knew this would be a tense visit for both of them, but wanted one last opportunity to bathe in the glow of Yuke's love.

Yuke arrived at three, as usual bearing pizza, and behaved as if it were an ordinary Friday. This was plainly an act for Mara's benefit. The best approach would be to talk about the elephant in the room. Sitting next to Yuke on the sofa, Mara stressed how positive she felt following her conversation with Claire.

"She gave me some useful information, and I honestly think I have a good chance of staying hidden for the whole week."

Mara was pretending to a confidence she didn't really feel, and Yuke obviously knew it. But for now, the pretence of optimism would have to substitute for the real thing. They followed their usual Friday routine - one long round of food, films and sex - and when they finally went to sleep in each other's arms, Mara realized that if she could not have a normal life at the moment, this counterfeit was nonetheless giving her something she needed.

The next day, Yuke suggested they go shopping, and though Mara felt more than usually reluctant to put on the uniform, she had to admit it would be nice to get out for a while. They caught the tube to Camden, and spent the afternoon looking around the market. On one stall they found a strange device that resembled the menu for an expensive restaurant, but which the seller, a man in his sixties, informed them was a Kindle. It contained, he explained, an electronic screen on which the text of a book could be read. Mara and Yuke couldn't understand why anyone would want to read a book on a screen when they could read it on paper, but the seller insisted it had been something of a fad many years ago, and he recalled his parents using one.

The facade of normality was maintained for the rest of the weekend, though Mara and Yuke's lovemaking had a frenzied desperation to it, as if they were clinging to each other for protection. When the time came to say goodbye, Mara tried to combine casualness with seriousness.

"We won't be seeing each other next weekend, but I'll call you as soon as the Hunt is over, so expect to hear from me on the afternoon of the 30th."

Neither of them needed to mention that it would be too painful for Yuke to accompany Mara to the stadium. After one last embrace, Yuke left to catch the last tube.

Mara hadn't informed her friends about the Hunt - though they were a tight group, it wasn't unusual not to hear from individual members for several weeks - but she felt they deserved to know. Aside from that, she wanted to make sure Yuke would have whatever support she needed. So on Monday morning, she wrote the following email:

```
From: Mara.Gorki@aol.com
Subject: The Hunt
Dear Friends
You are all very important to me, and I feel you
should know that I have been conscripted into the
Hunt. I will have to depart on Friday, and will be
gone for seven days. I will contact you as soon as
```

possible to let you know I am alright. While I'm
away, I'd greatly appreciate it if you would look
after Yuke. She is very upset, and will need
something to take her mind off things during my
absence. I look forward to seeing you when I get
back. xxx
    Mara.

Mara added the email addresses of her closest friends, the ones who knew how intimate her relationship with Yuke was, and hit 'send'. But she still felt something had been left undone. Deaths during the Hunt seemed relatively rare - she'd certainly never heard of one - but torture at the hands of a sexual sadist could hardly be described as a safe activity, no matter how many rules the sadist was obliged to follow. If she were to die during the Hunt, everything she owned would go to the state, or to a cousin she despised. Mara looked up the number of Madeleine Danes, the lawyer who'd handled her parents' estate, and made an appointment for Wednesday.

To Mara's relief, her cycle started that afternoon: her periods were erratic, and she'd been worried about having to deal with one during the Hunt. As far as she knew, women weren't even allowed to take sanitary towels into the arena. She spent the next two days editing *French Kill*, and had almost completed it when the time for her appointment with Madeleine arrived.

Madeleine Danes' practice was located above an antique store in Belsize Park, and hadn't changed since Mara last saw it seven years ago. Madeleine had been a friend of Mara's parents, so their relationship was not purely professional. She'd enjoyed a successful career as an actress before turning to the law, and her reception room contained framed photographs from stage productions with which she had been involved. One picture that caught Mara's eye showed Madeleine at the age of twelve playing the role of Nicky, a male character, in Harold Pinter's play *One for the Road*.

When Mara was ushered into Madeleine's office, the lawyer greeted her warmly. She'd always been favourably disposed towards Mara, and didn't raise an eyebrow at her decision to leave money and property to someone she described as a very close friend. Mara explained why she felt the need to make a will, and Madeleine nodded sympathetically.

"I don't think it's all that dangerous, but I understand why you want to be cautious."

As Madeleine escorted Mara out of the office, an arm affectionately resting on her shoulder, she added, "If anything happens, I'll make sure that this Yuke gets everything, and that anyone who makes unsupported allegations concerning the nature of her relationship with you finds themselves learning a great deal about our libel laws." Mara hardly knew how to respond, so she simply squeezed Madeleine's hand in gratitude and departed.

French Kill was completed the following day. While emailing it to her publisher, Mara decided not to say anything about the Hunt. She'd already begun receiving concerned phone calls from her friends, and though she was genuinely grateful for them, they made it harder to stay focused. She spent the evening listening to music, hoping Beethoven would give her the courage to endure her forthcoming ordeal. She found herself more moved than ever before by the Choral Symphony's progress from the darkly ominous to the purely joyous. It suggested a utopian vision emerging from a journey into the heart of darkness. After Beethoven came Mozart, whose music had always expressed to her what life might be like if it cast off the restrictions and repressions with which it was so frequently bound. This was the world as it perhaps could, and certainly should be. Tomorrow, she'd come face to face with the world as it currently was. As she slipped beneath her duvet around midnight, Mara couldn't help dwelling on the fact that the next time she climbed into this bed, she'd be a very different person. She recalled Catherine's horrified reaction to the sight of a woman being beaten, and her own more controlled response. Her sensibilities had already been brutalised. How much worse would they be after the Hunt? She'd coped surprisingly well during the last few days, but that night she cried herself to sleep.

Friday morning arrived all too quickly. Mara knew she'd have to leave at one-thirty in order to catch the tube. Remembering food would be hard to come by during the Hunt, she made a large lunch, and, despite having no appetite, forced herself to eat it. All she needed to bring with were the railcard, some spare change, and her phone. She wouldn't be able to take the phone into the arena, but she'd promised to call Yuke as soon as possible after the Hunt ended. At one-fifteen, Mara reluctantly removed the jeans and jumper she was wearing, already looking forward to the moment when she could change back into them. The process of donning the uniform was more than usually frustrating, since she'd be wearing it for several days. She found a new pair of tights, and after putting on the blouse and skirt, added the now obligatory jacket and stepped into the shoes. She was ready to depart. Casting a last fond glance around her apartment, with its reassuring stacks of books, Mara walked through the front door and closed it behind her. She was on her way to the Hunt.

BOOK 2
MARA GORKI
(DURING THE HUNT)

CHAPTER 7

Friday March 23rd

Mara arrived at Hunt tube station around two-twenty. She'd never visited this area before, even when it had been known as Kilburn, and was surprised to discover what in most respects looked like an ordinary London suburb, with rows of houses and shops full of customers. But there was no mistaking what those walls in the middle distance signified. Mara was supposed to present herself at the stadium between two-thirty and three. Not wanting to be early, she decided to go for a coffee in one of the nearby cafes. The waitress, who was presumably used to seeing Hunt participants arrive on Friday afternoons, smiled at her sympathetically. Mara spent ten minutes drinking a latte and attempting to steel herself. At two-thirty-five, she left the cafe and walked towards the stadium. Drawing closer, she saw a steel door with the words 'Hunt Stadium' emblazoned on it, and a buzzer situated beneath a 'ring for admission' sign. Mara could have gone in immediately, but it didn't appear anyone else had arrived yet, so she decided to walk around and try gauging the arena's size. The wall was approximately fifty feet in height, and curved inward at the top. Climbing it would be impossible.

Arriving back at the entrance, Mara noticed a car parked outside. A middle-aged couple were standing by the vehicle talking to a girl with long black hair who seemed too young to be wearing the uniform, let alone participating in a Hunt. Yet, as Mara approached the car, it became obvious she was witnessing parents seeing off their conscripted daughter. Mara felt for all of them: mother and father unable to contain their grief, daughter on the verge of hysteria. The parents were clearly making the girl's departure more stressful, and Mara decided to intervene. She held out her hand, saying, "Hi. My name's Mara. Shall we go in together?"

The girl calmed down, shook Mara's hand, and said, "I'm Julie. Yeah, I guess we'd better."

Julie hugged her parents one last time and walked towards the entrance with Mara, trying to ignore her mother's pleas. Mara felt almost angry with the woman. Did she think her daughter was entering the stadium by choice? Mara turned to Julie and smiled.

"Pretty scary, huh?"

Julie smiled back, relieved to hear she wasn't the only one who found this situation frightening. Mara rang the buzzer, and a few seconds later the door opened. It was obviously an automatic door which had been activated by somebody inside the building, but it made Mara think of those scenes in horror films where the portal of the haunted house mysteriously swings open, as if controlled by ghostly hands. She stepped inside, followed by Julie.

The two women found themselves standing in a reception room that wouldn't have looked out of place in a medical clinic. There were rows of chairs and a counter, behind which sat a female receptionist. Fighting back the urge to turn around and run, Mara approached the receptionist and said, "We're here for the Hunt." The woman indicated a scanner sitting on the counter and asked Mara to place her thumb on it. Mara tried to keep her hand from trembling as she pressed down on the screen.

After consulting a computer, the woman said, "Mara Gorki, welcome to the Hunt. If you have any personal belongings, please hand them over." Mara removed the phone, loose change and railcard from her jacket pocket. The receptionist sealed these items in a plastic bag which she deposited in a cubbyhole. "Take a seat and wait for your name to be called," she said before gesturing to Julie and going through the same routine with the scanner. "Julie Weisz, welcome to the Hunt," she declared before collecting Julie's belongings. When asked to take a seat, Julie hesitantly selected the chair next to Mara, as if fearing her presence might be unwelcome. Julie's nervousness was actually helping Mara control her own fear, and she gave the girl's hand a reassuring squeeze.

"How you feeling?" she asked.

"I've never been so scared. Oh God, I don't want to do this!"

Mara leaned over and whispered, "Stay close to me. I know a few things that might help us." Julie looked at Mara with something approaching awe. She was obviously eager to hear more, but Mara, who didn't want to risk being overheard, shook her head and mouthed the word 'later'. After a few minutes of silence, Julie asked the receptionist if she could use the toilet. The woman pointed at a restroom located to the right of the counter, and Julie walked quickly towards it.

After Julie left, three women were buzzed in almost immediately. Mara heard the receptionist identify them as Anne Radford, Susan Anderson and Zong Xifeng. Zong, an attractive Chinese woman, sat down next to Mara, while Anne and Susan took separate seats and looked around without saying anything. "Are you nervous?" asked Zong, adding, "I'm terrified."

"I'm sure we all are," replied Mara, turning her head so she could see the other new arrivals: Anne, a blonde in her late twenties, was sitting on her hands, while Susan, who appeared to be Mara's age, repeatedly crossed, uncrossed and recrossed her legs. Mara was struck by her waist length hair, though she couldn't help thinking it would be a liability in a chase. Mara approached Anne, and as the two women shook hands, Mara asked how she was doing.

"I'm scared shitless," responded Anne, "though hopefully I won't have to participate. I'm a standby." Mara wasn't familiar with this term, so Anne explained: "Sometimes women who are drafted into the Hunt obtain medical exemptions, or simply don't turn up on the day, so there are always a few standbys. Like a theatrical understudy," she added with a wry smile.

The buzzer sounded again, and a woman with her hands cuffed behind her back stumbled through the door. She was followed by two male police officers. As this group approached the counter, one of the officers unlocked the handcuffs, enabling his charge to place her thumb on the scanner. "Isabella Braschi, welcome to the Hunt," said the receptionist. Isabella had no personal belongings, and when told to take a seat, she grabbed a chair in the front row while her guardians positioned themselves by the stadium door, watching her attentively.

Mara and Anne moved forwards and introduced themselves. Isabella shook their hands and said, "As you can probably guess, I'm a Hunt Evader."

"How'd they find you?" asked Anne sympathetically.

"I don't really know," sighed Isabella. "I couldn't face the prospect of participating in a Hunt, so when I was conscripted I decided to run. A friend in Brighton let me stay with her. I was hiding in the attic, just like Anne Frank. But after I'd been there two months, I had to get out, so I started taking walks along the front. One day, the police followed me back to the house and arrested me. I was probably detected by some kind of facial recognition technology. That was three weeks ago, and I've been in a cell ever since. Now I'll have to take part in a Hunt anyway, and when it's over, I'll be sent straight back to prison. The court sentenced me to five years, and the woman who hid me got one year." Isabella began sobbing, and Anne gently rubbed her back.

Julie had been gone several minutes, and Mara was starting to worry. While Anne did her best to comfort Isabella, Mara went into the restroom, where she found Julie bent over a toilet, attempting to vomit. Mara stroked her hair and said, "I know it's awful, but we'll have to be brave." As she said this, Mara remembered her interview with Catherine, during which she'd insisted she was not a brave person. Could she be brave now? She supposed she didn't have any choice. Julie wiped her face with toilet paper and followed Mara back into the reception room. During their absence, the remaining women had arrived, and were being processed. Mara didn't catch their names. She sat down next to Isabella, who seemed calmer, and introduced Julie.

One of the new arrivals, a short woman with spiky black hair, flopped down next to them. "I'm Kate Mackendrick," she proclaimed sardonically, "and I don't want to be here." Noting the woman's accent, Mara asked if she'd travelled from Scotland. Kate proudly declared herself to be a native of Glasgow, and complained of how exhausted she felt after the five-hour train journey.

Mara was about to say hello to the others when the receptionist shouted, "Anne Radford. Rachel Kahn. We won't be needing you today, so you may leave whenever you wish." Anne and one of the women who had just arrived jumped up, expressions of relief on their faces. Anne's happiness quickly turned to embarrassment as she regarded her less fortunate companions.

"I...I'm sorry that I...I..."

Mara grasped her hand. "I'm not," she insisted. "I'm glad you're getting out of this." They embraced each other, and after collecting her belongings, Anne left without saying another word, waving weakly as she did so.

No sooner had the two standbys departed than a door to the left of the reception counter opened and a man wearing a grey suit entered. After consulting the receptionist, he approached the seating area and clapped his hands for silence, something he received immediately. "Ladies," he announced to the ten draftees, who were giving him their full attention, "thank you for arriving on time, and welcome to the Hunt. Please follow me." The women followed their escort into a narrow corridor, where he took a quick head count and said, "In a moment, we will proceed to the room in which you will interact with the Hunters. But first, please line up with your backs against the wall." Once the women were in position, the escort moved down the line, carefully frisking each of them in turn. Mara resented being fondled so intimately by this stranger, who even raised her skirt and ran his hands over her crotch and backside, but there seemed little point protesting. Unless she was very lucky, this would be the least of the indignities she'd be subjected to over the next few days. Satisfied nobody was concealing anything, the man opened a door at the corridor's end and said, "Ladies, please enter the meeting area."

The room they were shown into looked like a provincial dancehall, a resemblance underlined by the presence of ten men standing in a row by the opposite wall, as if awaiting the appearance of their dance partners. They struck Mara as an unimpressive bunch. Physically they ranged from the razor thin to the absurdly fat, and while some were well groomed, others looked like they'd fallen out of bed a few minutes ago and so far failed to locate a comb. Mara thought they had an air of malevolence; not unsurprisingly, given that they'd paid large sums of money for the privilege of abusing young women. One especially obese man actually licked his lips. Most of the men were wearing loose-fitting jeans or tracksuit trousers. All of them wore trainers. Clothes that allowed for rapid movement. Mara glanced at her fellow conscripts in their knee-length skirts and court shoes. She had difficulty imagining them outrunning even the fattest of the men.

As he closed the door, the escort cheerfully said, "Ladies, gentlemen, please mingle."

For at least two minutes, neither group moved: the women nervously shuffled their feet, while the men consulted each other, pointing at the women and talking intensely, as if trying to agree on something. It occurred to Mara that, in their way, the Hunters were as nervous as the hunted. Finally, several members of the male group approached the female group, and the rest soon followed. The one Mara had seen licking his lips came up to her, said, "Hello, I'm Simon," and initiated a handshake with his right hand while grasping Mara's forearm with his left. This struck her as a curiously friendly gesture under the circumstances. "Hope we get to know each other better," he grunted.

Mara couldn't think of an appropriate response - 'Yeah, I'd love to be raped and tortured by you' didn't have the right ring to it - so she attempted a smile and said, "Sure." Appearing to take this as a sign of encouragement, Simon shuffled away, grinning at her over his shoulder. Seeing these men up close, she was struck by how much they reminded her of the sadistic boys who had tormented her on the train. It was nothing she could put her finger on, just a certain look in the eyes, a certain way of moving.

Several of the Hunters walked silently past Mara, running their eyes over her as if she were a piece of meat. Aside from Simon, only one man - not attractive, but at least relatively clean - actually addressed her. He didn't offer to shake hands, but instead looked her directly in the face and said, "I'd like to make a deal with you. I assume you've seen the list of things I'm permitted to do." Mara hadn't expected such a direct acknowledgement of the Hunt's reality at this point, but she nodded. "Okay," said the man, "if you turn yourself over to me at the beginning of the Hunt, I'll let you select four items from that list to be declared off-limits." Mara could hardly believe she was hearing this, and the shock was evident on her face. "No need to make up your mind now," continued the man. "If you decide to accept my offer, be waiting outside the Hunters' apartment block when I arrive there, which will be a little over an hour after you enter the arena. If you don't turn up, pray I'm not the one who catches you." He walked away without waiting for an answer, and stood by the wall staring at her.

Mara was appalled, but also tempted. The thought of being pierced with needles terrified her more than anything else, and if she accepted this bizarre offer, she could rule out the possibility of that happening. What else could she rule out? As Mara's mind raced through the items on the list, she happened to see one of the better dressed men shaking Zong's hand in the same way Simon had shaken hers, grasping the forearm as he did so. That seemed curious. Might it be some kind of sign, like a Masonic handshake? She kept an eye on what was happening elsewhere in the room, and soon noticed two more men exchanging similar handshakes with Kate and one of the women whose names she hadn't heard. What was it Claire had said? "I remembered him because the creep shook my hand and said he looked forward to getting to know me...He was strolling along, calm as you please, scrutinising a handheld device...he seemed to be paying close attention to it...I don't know how, but he'd found some way of tracking me...the creep shook my hand."

Mara shuddered. She felt certain these men were planting tracking devices on their chosen victims. That must have been what they were discussing so intensely. She desperately wanted to examine the forearm of her jacket, but didn't dare. She'd have to wait until they were in the arena. As if on cue, their escort again clapped his hands and shouted, "Gentlemen, I'm afraid you must now bid the ladies goodbye, at least for a while." The men obediently walked away; Mara thought some of them even looked a little relieved. "Ladies," announced the escort, "it is time for you to enter the arena. Please follow me."

The women were conducted through a door positioned to the left of the meeting hall, and down an anonymous corridor which led to a room containing nothing but an iron gate. To Mara, this room, with its blank walls and white floor, had a chilling aura of finality. For some reason, it reminded her of a passage from Dostoyevsky's *Crime and Punishment* that she'd never managed to get out of her head: "We always imagine eternity as something beyond our conception, something vast, vast! But why must it be vast? Instead of all that, what if it's one little room, like a bath-house in the country, black and grimy and spiders in every corner, and that's all eternity is? I sometimes fancy it like that."

Stopping before the gate, the escort turned around and waited until the women were assembled in front of him. He addressed them in a solemn voice.

"Ladies, in a moment you will pass through this gate and into the arena. The Hunt will begin as soon as the gate is closed behind you. At one p.m. next Friday, an alarm audible throughout the arena will be sounded for five minutes. If you have not been caught by then, you may return to the gate. Does anyone have any questions?"

The women looked around nervously, but nobody said anything. "Very well," said the escort, glancing at his watch. "It is three-fifty-two. You may now enter. The Hunters will be allowed in at precisely four-fifty-two." Turning around, he grasped a handle on the gate, and pulled it towards him. As the gate slowly opened, the man stood aside. The women were plainly reluctant to move, and Mara decided to go first. Once they were safe from prying eyes and ears, she needed to have a serious conversation with her companions, and it would be best to establish herself as leader. Taking a deep breath, she marched through the gate.

Although what confronted Mara on the other side was pretty much what her conversation with Claire had led her to expect, actually seeing it was something else. She stood at the end of what had once been Kilburn High Road, but was now home to the decaying remnants of shops, bars and restaurants. Apartments located above these businesses were mostly hollow shells, their exterior walls long gone, exposing the crumbling interiors like a dollhouse with its front opening removed. The looted and burned skeletons of cars littered the road. Mara could see rats scattering in all directions at the sight of human activity. She heard the gate shut, and turned around to see the nine other women standing by it, looking about apprehensively. Mara could easily imagine them behaving the way Claire's group had, remaining in one spot until the Hunters arrived. There wasn't a moment to spare. Mara addressed the women in a loud voice.

"Everyone, please listen to me. I know a few things which might help us survive. The first thing I need to find out is how many of you remember one of the Hunters shaking your hand."

Mara noticed Julie was standing next to her, as if afraid to lose sight of the woman she regarded as her protectress. Mara smiled at Julie and grabbed her right arm with both hands, demonstrating the curious handshake she'd received from Simon.

"Do any of you recall a Hunter touching you like this, with his left hand clasping your right forearm?"

Everyone nodded, and Mara was amused to see the women gazing at her as if she were the answer to their prayers. Given the situation they were in, anyone willing to assume a leadership role was evidently more than welcome to do so.

"Okay," continued Mara, taking off her jacket. "I have reason to believe the Hunters planted tracking devices on us. If I'm right, they'll have attached these devices to our jackets. So the first thing we need to do is locate and remove them." Mara examined her jacket. At first she found nothing on the sleeve. Could she have been wrong? Was the handshake merely symbolic? She placed the garment on the ground and ran her fingers along its sleeve, slowly covering every inch, intensely aware she might be wasting valuable time. But there it was. A black speck, so small she initially thought it nothing more than a spot of dirt. It came off with one sharp tug. Mara placed it on the end of her index finger. Only by close inspection could she confirm that it was indeed an electronic device. This, presumably, was why the Hunt authorities insisted on female participants wearing their uniform jackets. On a white blouse, the device might have been visible, but on a black jacket it couldn't possibly be discovered unless somebody were specifically searching for it.

Mara held up her finger and said, "This is what you're looking for. When you find one, be careful not to lose it." Precious minutes passed before every device was located, but eventually all ten women held the trackers in their hands. Mara grinned as she addressed them.

"We don't have much time, but I'll tell you everything I know. The Hunters can trace these trackers, but don't assume they'll be relying on them. They have machines which detect body heat, but only within a limited range. So you'll need to find tall buildings, and go as high as possible. That way, they can only detect you by entering the building and walking up to your floor. If that happens, you'll need to run. They also have infra-red goggles that allow them to see at night, so stay inside after dark, otherwise you'll be sitting ducks. They're armed with Tasers, and if they touch you with one, you'll be knocked out. If they catch you, they might lock a collar around your neck and tell you they can use a remote control to immobilise you even from a mile away. I'm assured this is not a bluff. I know your instinct is to stay together, but that'll make it easier for them to find you, so we need to split up, at least into groups of two. That way, one person can stand guard while the other sleeps. We should all head off in different directions. But before we do that, I have an idea which will hopefully confuse the Hunters. After you leave this area, drop your tracker into one of the drains along the sides of the roads. They'll flow into the sewer, and if the Hunters can still detect them, they might think we've found a way to hide underground, and waste their time working out how to get down there. But don't drop the tracker anywhere near the place you're hiding, and don't forget to take food and drink from a vending machine."

Mara felt pleased with this speech. She'd summed up all the important points, and her audience was visibly impressed. "Does anyone have any questions?" she asked, in a parody of their escort's masculine voice. The women laughed, but already they were splitting up into twos and waving gratefully at her.

As Mara put her jacket back on, Julie approached apprehensively and asked, "Would you mind if I come with you?"

Mara was touched by the look on the girl's face. Julie couldn't have been more than four years her junior, yet apparently regarded her as a mother figure. Mara realised she'd more or less accepted this role, and had been thinking of Julie as a 'girl': she was almost certainly the youngest person there, and the circumstances of their first meeting made Mara feel protective towards her. She smiled at Julie and said, "We'll look out for each other."

Watches were not permitted in the arena, so there was no way of knowing precisely how much time had passed, but Mara thought they still had at least forty minutes before the Hunters arrived. The other women were already on the move, and Mara began striding rapidly down the main road, gesturing for Julie to follow. Walking as quickly as possible, they passed a church which Mara briefly considered using as a hiding place: its upper floors were certainly high enough, and even an atheist can be moved by the impulse to seek sanctuary in such a construction. But it was too close to the gate, and also perhaps too obvious. So they turned off to the left, and started exploring the network of side streets: Mara instructed Julie to drop her tracker down a drain in one of them, and disposed of her own soon afterwards.

The landscape through which they passed held a grim fascination. Mara knew Kilburn had been effectively abandoned during the forties due to multiple bank repossessions, but she couldn't account for the sheer scale of destruction. As Claire had observed, the area resembled a war zone. Some buildings appeared to have been partially torn down or blown apart, yet right next to them were places that seemed comparatively pristine. One store even had an unbroken window on which the words 'Do your fresh shop here' could be deciphered. The store itself was empty. As Mara and Julie turned a corner, a vending machine stood out amidst the wreckage, and they stopped to take sandwiches and bottles of water from it, placing the items in their jacket pockets. They were moving in the direction of some large apartment buildings which looked relatively intact, at least from a distance.

There turned out to be six such buildings, each approximately twenty storeys high, arranged around a grassy square that had seen better days. It had presumably once been used for recreational purposes, but was now an impenetrable jungle. Observed up close, the buildings themselves were much the worse for wear: one was leaning at a sharp angle - Mara immediately thought of it as the Leaning Tower of Kilburn - and gave the impression that it would eventually topple and knock over the next building, perhaps bringing down all six like a row of dominoes. A particular block caught Mara's eye. The apartments on its lower floors were heavily damaged, but those higher up appeared relatively unscathed. The Hunters would undoubtedly be in the arena by now - Mara wished she could see their faces when they tried locating the trackers - and it would be dark soon, so this was as good a place as any to spend the night. The building had no front door, so they cautiously entered, discovering a lobby filled with tattered furniture, empty cans, piles of mattresses, and various unidentifiable objects. Since they weren't wearing the most appropriate attire in which to negotiate such an obstacle course, they progressed slowly towards the staircase on the far side of the lobby. There were flies everywhere, and the building was infested with rats. Even the stairs were filthy, with more junk to clamber over or push aside on every landing. Former occupants would have relied on elevators, but there had been no electricity here for a decade. The smell on the lower floors was awful, but as they gradually ascended, the air seemed to become clearer. Perhaps they were simply growing used to it. Upon reaching the top floor, they left the stairwell and entered a corridor, choking on the clouds of dust they stirred up with every step. Stopping in front of a randomly selected apartment, Mara tried to open the door, which was locked. By kicking at the flimsy wooden structure's base, the two women forced their way in.

The apartment contained nothing except bare walls and empty rooms. Mara assumed nobody had been there since the forties. It wouldn't be the most comfortable place to hide out, but they were unlikely to be discovered unless a Hunter decided to go from floor to floor trying to detect body heat. Mara and Julie took turns relieving themselves in the bathroom. There was no water, not even in the toilet bowl, so they'd have to make the bottles from the vending machine last. Doing their best to ignore the dust, they sat on the floor and leaned against a wall, holding each other for comfort and warmth. It was already growing dark, and Mara wondered what Yuke would say if she knew her lover planned to spend the night in another woman's arms. The thought made her chuckle. Yuke would be delighted to learn Mara was okay.

Julie seemed reluctant to say anything unless asked a direct question, so Mara tried drawing her out.

"Tell me something about yourself. How old are you? You don't look old enough to be drafted."

"I'm almost not," responded Julie. "I only turned twenty-one three months ago."

"You barely look eighteen."

"I know. I still wear my own clothes sometimes, and nobody ever checks my ID. I realise I'm taking a risk, but I hate skirts."

"Me too. But you should be careful. I was caned for going out in jeans."

"I have a cousin who escaped from Israel, and she told me that after the ultra-Orthodox took over, women weren't even allowed to wear trousers in their own homes. The religious police could enter any time to make sure they were properly dressed. Women are banned from reading novels and singing in public there as well. I love reading and I'm a singer, so on the whole I'd rather live here, despite the Hunt."

"I'd never have guessed you were a singer."

"I become a different person onstage. My boyfriend has a band called Get to Know Your Rabbit. I sing with them, and wrote one of their songs. We don't have a recording deal yet, but we're getting a lot of club bookings."

"Do you live in London?"

"Yeah. I live with my parents in Ealing, but I'm hoping to move in with my boyfriend later this year. Where do you live?"

"Caledonian Road. It's near St. Pancras."

"St. Pancras is great. We performed in a club there once."

"How about singing your song for me?"

"You need to hear it with the music."

Mara made a comical pleading face and said, "Oh pleeease!"

Julie couldn't help laughing. "Okay, but it really won't be the same." She leaned back, closed her eyes, and began humming. Then one of the most exquisite voices Mara had ever heard filled the dark apartment.

There is a house on the edge of town.
It's been there forever, so they say.
I've never once been inside it,
Though I pass it every single day.

My friends all believe it's haunted
By ghosts and spirits of the past.
But the only ghosts I'm afraid of
Are those of a life that will not last.

I know some day I must enter this house,
And leave behind everything that's me.
But until then I think I'll keep passing by,

Trying to pretend that I am free."

Mara was moved to tears. "That's beautiful. But it's so sad."

"Yet I'm not a sad person," said Julie, more to herself than to Mara. She shook her head, as if suddenly remembering where she was. "Well, I am at the moment, but not normally."

"What does the house represent? Death?"

"It could be. But it's more than that. Loss of identity, loss of individuality. Death is the ultimate loss of individuality."

"You say one day you must enter the house. Does that mean you see loss of individuality as inevitable, even before death?"

"I guess so. It's hard for me to explain. I'm much better at expressing these things in lyrics and poems."

Mara hesitated a moment before asking, "Are we in the house now?"

"No...not yet...I don't know. Let's talk about something else. What do you do?"

"I write too, actually. I'm a novelist."

Julie was excited by this. "Should I have heard of you?"

"Of course you should," said Mara with a grin. "But you won't have done. All my books are banned by the British censor."

"Why?"

"They're about a female private detective named Melissa Valance. The powers that be don't like books which show women acting independently. I suppose they think it might give people the wrong idea about our place in society."

"I don't understand why men hate women so much in this country. I'm sure it's not like that everywhere. It didn't even used to be like that here."

"I think it was always like this, here and most other places. It's all on the surface now. But if you study history, you'll find misogyny existed in some form at all periods. I have a friend who's a film critic. She once showed me Ingmar Bergman's *The Serpent's Egg*. It's set in Germany during the nineteen-twenties, and there's a scene where a character claims that anyone willing to make the slightest effort could see what was going to happen in the next decade, the Nazi era. He says it's like a serpent's egg. Through the thin membranes you can clearly discern the already perfect reptile. Everyone thinks Britain was so civilised earlier this century. But there's never been any shortage of politicians wanting to control women's bodies. Abortion was legal for a while, but conservative MPs were constantly trying to restrict abortion rights, and they finally won the battle. Abortion was never legalised in Ireland. Even the uniform isn't a new idea. In some places, women had to wear abayas or burquas which completely covered their faces whenever they left home. And back then, there was something called Female Genital Mutilation. Do you know what that is?"

Julie shook her head.

"It's almost unbelievable. Certain parents - motivated by vague notions of religion, honour and tradition - would make their daughters take part in ceremonies where they were forcibly restrained while a razor blade was used to remove their clitoris, inner labia and outer labia. Parents who were particularly religious, honourable or traditional demonstrated these qualities by obliging girls - who had absolutely no say in the matter - to undergo infibulation. After everything had been cut away, whatever skin remained was stretched across the vagina and stitched together, leaving only a small hole for urine and menstrual blood. All this was usually done without anaesthetic. Technically the practice was illegal, but it had the tacit approval of the British authorities. Thousands of women were mutilated every year, but there wasn't a single prosecution. The Hunt seems almost mild by comparison. The most these bastards are allowed to do is pierce us with needles."

"You don't think they'd really do anything like that, though, do you? I read the Hunt pamphlet, but I can't believe they'd actually do those things."

"I think we need to be as careful as possible not to let them find us."

Julie removed the bottle of water from her pocket and took a drink. Mara couldn't see clearly in the dark, but after Julie replaced the cap and placed the bottle on the floor, Mara picked it up and shook it. From the sound, she guessed it was almost empty. She desperately wanted a drink herself, but the deviousness of the Hunt planners' scheme was now becoming apparent to her. Food and particularly drink were essential to survival, yet women taking part in the Hunt could only use a vending machine every six hours, obtaining just a single food item and a single drink item. And these small packages provided little more than token nourishment or refreshment. So even if a woman managed to remove her tracking device and find a relatively safe hiding place, she'd still need to go outside and use a vending machine at least once a day. And the Hunters would undoubtedly be staking out these machines, waiting for potential victims. Throw body heat detectors, infra-red goggles and Tasers into the mix, and a cynic might conclude that the decks in this particular game were not stacked in the women's favour.

Mara picked up her own bottle of water. Turning to Julie she said, "We need to make the water last as long as possible. I'm going to have a small sip now, and we can share the rest tomorrow morning." Julie nodded: she didn't have to be reminded what was at stake. Mara took the smallest sip possible, but even that drained more than a third of the contents. Reluctantly putting the bottle's cap securely back on, she set it down near where they were sitting. Neither woman felt particularly hungry, so the sandwiches remained in their pockets.

After a few minutes of silence, Mara stood up and looked out the window. The streets were dark, though lighted windows in the Hunters' apartment block, the one building with electricity, could be seen in the distance. Mara wondered if any of her comrades had already been caught, and were undergoing torture at that very moment. Perhaps the Hunters were still running around like headless chickens trying to work out how their designated victims had managed to penetrate the sewer system. The thought made her smile. She'd suggested splitting up into groups of two so one person could stand guard, but there was obviously no point staring out the window all night, since nothing could be seen down below. She returned to Julie, who had fallen asleep. The girl's body had probably responded to her fear by shutting down and providing some much needed rest. Mara sat on the floor and laid Julie's head on her shoulder, being careful not to disturb her. She didn't expect to get any sleep, but it was a relief to be resting quietly. She regretted having referred to Yuke as a friend. She trusted Julie, but suspected the girl would feel uncomfortable being in close physical proximity to someone who might desire her sexually. In truth, Mara's feelings towards Julie were purely protective. But she really must stop thinking of her as 'the girl'. Julie was no child and would need the strength of an adult to cope with this ordeal. On that thought, Mara drifted into a deep sleep.

CHAPTER 8

Saturday March 24th

Mara awoke soon after the sun rose. Julie had somehow ended up with her head on Mara's lap, and Mara decided to let her sleep a little longer, relishing the calm atmosphere, however false she knew it to be. She longed for a drink, but was determined to at least wait until Julie had woken up. After half an hour, Julie began to stir. Mara noticed she was smiling, and guessed that, in this state of half sleep, she'd forgotten where she was. Unsurprisingly, the smile vanished, and was replaced by a look of tension as reality came flooding in. Mara stroked Julie's hair and said, "Good morning," as the girl opened her eyes.

Julie sat up and said, "Good morning," in return, then asked, "Can I have some water?"

Mara reached for the bottle, saying, "This is all we have left. I'll drink half, then you drink half. After that, we'll need to find more." She opened the bottle and carefully took a sip before lowering it. It barely quenched her thirst - what must it be like taking part in a Hunt during the hot days of summer? - but she was pleased to see plenty remained for Julie. The girl accepted the bottle gratefully: she obviously felt guilty about so quickly exhausting her own supply. They were both hungry, and rapidly devoured the pathetically small sandwiches.

Mara walked back to the window. Now that the sun was up, she could see the street below. This was the first time she'd realised that the window of their apartment faced the rear rather than the front of the building. An identical apartment block was located directly opposite, on the other side of the wide street, a vending machine positioned near its entrance. Mara pointed out the machine to Julie, who volunteered to go down and bring back food and drink. Mara shook her head. "If anything, we'll go down together. That way we can take two bottles."

Julie looked Mara in the eyes, a rare sign of assertiveness. "If we go out together, there's a greater chance we'll both be caught. If I go alone, you can keep watch from the window and signal me in case of danger. We can easily last until tomorrow on one bottle of water and one sandwich, and then it'll be your turn to go outside."

Mara had to admit this plan made sense, so she reluctantly agreed. "But first," she suggested, "let's see what we can find in this building. If we're lucky, we might come across some old bottles of water. They won't taste good, but they should be drinkable." They decided Julie would search the floor they were occupying while Mara explored the one below.

As she entered the stairwell, Mara peered nervously over the banisters. She had no intention of becoming complacent. Walking as quietly as possible, she descended to the nineteenth floor. She tried every apartment, paying particularly close attention to the ones that were still locked. But forcing open even such flimsy doors was hard work, and she found only dust behind them. At least the rooms whose doors had already been forced showed signs of human activity, such as old newspapers, empty cans, and a couple of pillows. There were no liquids of any kind, nor anything edible. Mara picked up the pillows: they were filthy, but would make sleeping on the floor more comfortable. Continuing the search seemed pointless, so she returned to the top floor and found Julie walking empty-handed out of a room at the corridor's end. Her quest had proved equally fruitless.

Back inside the apartment, Mara had to admit it would be necessary to risk using the vending machine. She insisted on first standing by the window staring at the street for half an hour, looking for signs of Hunter activity. So far as she could see, the area was deserted. She once again offered to be the first to venture outside, but Julie was determined to accept this responsibility. Eventually, they decided to play rock-paper-scissors, and Julie's scissors beat Mara's paper.

That left only the question of signalling. Picking up one of the pillows she'd collected, Mara told Julie, "It should take you about twenty minutes to go down the stairs and across the lobby. If I don't see any Hunters during that time, I'll throw this pillow out the window and into the road in front of the vending machine. When you walk around the corner of this building, take a look at the road. If you don't see the pillow, that means there's danger, and you should come back immediately."

Julie agreed this was a good plan, and after giving Mara a hug she left the apartment. Mara took up her position by the window and scrutinised the street. It looked safe, but appearances in the arena could be deceptive. She had no way of accurately determining when twenty minutes had passed, but once she'd given Julie enough time to make her way downstairs, she opened the window, took one last look around, and threw out the pillow. It landed almost directly in front of the vending machine. A few seconds later, Julie came into view and walked across the road. Mara felt sick with fear.

Julie approached the vending machine, applied her thumb to its credit screen, and pressed a button. As she did this, she turned around and looked up, giving Mara a cheerful wave. And that's when it happened. A man emerged from behind the machine, Taser in one hand, steel collar in the other. He must have been waiting there for hours. Mara saw him before Julie did, and the image would haunt her for the rest of her life. She was too far away to make out Julie's face clearly, but her imagination filled in the big friendly smile that showed no knowledge of the monster looming up in the background. It was like seeing Red Riding Hood about to be devoured by the wolf.

Mara had never felt so powerless. No matter how quickly she moved, by the time she reached the ground floor the drama playing out below would be long over. She watched helplessly as Julie looked back and discovered the Hunter standing before her. Mara expected Julie to run, but the girl was frozen in terror. The man waved his Taser in Julie's face while holding out the collar to her, and though Mara couldn't hear what he was saying, it was obviously a variation on what Claire recalled a Hunter telling her: We can do this the hard way or we can do it the easy way. Julie took the collar and locked it on her neck. The man checked it was secure, then pointed towards the Hunters' block. At his bidding, Julie walked down the street, the Hunter following closely behind.

Mara slumped against the wall under the window, buried her face in her hands and screamed. She'd wanted to protect Julie, yet less than twenty-four hours after their first encounter, the girl had already been ensnared by one of those sadistic monsters. What made it worse was that Mara thought she recognised the Hunter. She couldn't be certain after only seeing him from such a distance, but she strongly suspected Julie's captor was Mr. Let's-Make-a-Deal, the creep who'd suggested Mara pray not to be caught by him.

Mara wept for an hour before attempting to pull herself together. One fact she couldn't ignore was that the Hunter must have seen Julie waving to somebody in the building opposite. Though he now had what he wanted, it seemed reasonable to assume he'd tell one of the other Hunters where fresh prey might be located. Without even formulating a coherent plan, Mara walked out of the apartment and began descending the stairs, moving as fast as possible. She reached the ground floor in fifteen minutes, and slowly made her way across the lobby. Once she was out in the open, her instinct for self-preservation told her that, whatever she did next, she should first obtain supplies. It seemed unlikely that two Hunters would stake out the same location, and Mara didn't anticipate any unwelcome encounters, but she still edged cautiously around the building before running across the street towards the vending machine. The bottle of water Julie had selected was still sitting in the open compartment. Mara considered leaving it there, but that was foolishness. Julie would have wanted her to have it. She put the bottle in her pocket, then placed her thumb on the scanner and purchased another bottle, as well as a sandwich. Walking back to the front of the building she'd just left, Mara looked around at the five other apartment blocks. She'd have liked to go somewhere completely different, but every minute spent outside increased the likelihood of her being spotted. The furthest building was the Leaning Tower of Kilburn, but the block next door seemed sturdy enough, and the possibility of the Leaning Tower collapsing on top of it provided the structure with an aura of danger that might deter Hunters. Giving a wide berth to the grassy square, which could conceal any number of threats, both human and animal, Mara moved as quickly as possible towards the next edifice in which she hoped to take refuge.

The block chosen by Mara actually had a front door, or at least the remains of one. Pushing it open, she saw a lobby which was similar to the one in the building she'd just left, but much easier to cross. Mara merely had to push aside a few cardboard boxes - she looked inside one, and found it contained plastic forks - as she made her way to the stairwell. While climbing the stairs, she couldn't stop thinking about Julie. The girl would have been inside the Hunters' apartment block for some time now, and might already be suffering in one of those hellish playrooms. The idea was intolerable, and when Mara reached the eighth floor, she sat on the stairs and cried again. As she resumed her journey up the stairwell, Mara realised that at no point had she seen any graffiti. It struck her as almost sad. Graffiti was an admittedly crude but nonetheless heartfelt expression of creativity and the need to communicate, and its absence suggested how thoroughly these basic human needs had been eradicated.

Mara decided to stop on the seventeenth floor. It was high enough to offer some protection from Hunters armed with body heat detectors, but a less obvious hiding place than the top floor. She left the stairwell and walked along a corridor containing the usual mix of apartments which had been occupied by transients before the area was sealed off, and locked doors that doubtless guarded nothing but dirty floors. Mara wanted a room from which she could observe the front of the building, so she turned a corner and headed towards the opposite corridor, stopping randomly at Apartment 1708, which appeared to be locked. As she prepared to force her way in, Mara grasped the doorknob and, almost by instinct, turned it. The door swung open.

But if Mara was surprised to find a door that had neither been locked nor broken, she was far more surprised when she walked through it. For she was now standing in what appeared to be a fully furnished apartment. In the living room were a sofa, comfortable chairs, and a table. In the bedroom, a bed with duvet neatly turned back, a wooden chair, and a bedside table, as well as a large wardrobe filled with clothes - everything from expensive dresses to children's shoes. The kitchen included a washing machine and a fridge, both empty. The bathroom contained a dry toilet and a bath, next to which had been placed a towel and a bottle of shampoo. Everything was covered in dust, some of it inches thick. It was as if somebody's home had been preserved under a protective grey layer so future generations could see how people used to live.

But the biggest surprise, and the one that made Mara wonder if she'd responded to the strain of the last twenty-four hours by retreating into some kind of fantasy, was the books. They not only filled several shelves, but were stacked against every wall, just as they were in Mara's own apartment. Inspecting the stacks, Mara discovered the selection was impossibly eclectic. Celebrity biographies rubbed shoulders with classics of world literature, an anthology of bad taste jokes with a history of the Russian Revolution. Most of the books were in English, but Mara noticed a few in Polish and Italian, and some in languages she didn't recognise. On top of one shelf, in a prominent position, was a sealed envelope with the words, "A letter from Mary Green, to whoever currently occupies Apt. 1708," neatly written on it.

Mara returned to the front door and shut it carefully. There was no doubt in her mind that unless circumstances forced her to leave, this was where she'd be spending the rest of the week. Taking the sandwich and the water bottles out of her pockets, she placed them on the living room table and calculated whether she could make the water last until Friday. It would mean drinking no more than one third of a bottle each day. Difficult, but not impossible. The lack of food didn't especially worry her. She could easily go for a week without eating. And she hadn't yet searched the kitchen cupboards. There might be cans of food that were still edible. She tried turning the taps to see if anything happened - nothing would have surprised her now - but the water supply had obviously been cut off years ago. Looking inside one of the cabinets over the sink, she discovered various cleaning utensils. The cabinet next to it was empty. Disappointed, she opened the cupboard next to the washing machine, and found two boxes. Pulling back the cardboard flaps, she gasped. The first box contained six bottles of wine. She eagerly opened the second box, which contained another six bottles.

Mara seriously wondered if she were asleep and dreaming. The apartment might have been custom-made for her. If only she'd come across this place earlier, in time to share it with Julie. How she longed to have the girl there: Mara could picture her face lighting up at the sight of the wine.

She arranged the bottles on a plastic surface that divided the kitchen from the living room. There were six bottles of white wine and six of red. Mara would have to be careful, since she'd be spending a week imbibing nothing but alcohol on an empty stomach. It occurred to her that this was undoubtedly how a lot of 'real' - which is to say male - writers lived. She opened a bottle of white, threw her head back, and poured a little wine into her mouth. It tasted good. She took another swallow and replaced the lid. She didn't want to get drunk, at least not right away.

Returning to the bedroom, Mara rummaged through the wardrobe's contents and pulled out a faded pair of jeans which seemed to be her size. They'd be more comfortable than her skirt, and more practical if she needed to run. She also found a pair of battered trainers, some socks, and a thick jumper. The latter was too big for her, but would provide protection against the cold. After removing her clothes and depositing them neatly on the chair, she put on the jeans, which fit perfectly, the jumper and the socks. The trainers were a little tight, but otherwise fine. Mara wondered if she could get into trouble for being out of uniform here, especially if she left the apartment. The arena wasn't exactly a public place, and the uniform exemption for women participating in sporting events might apply. In any case, there were no police around to report her, and if everything went according to plan, she'd simply change back before departing on Friday. Pulling the duvet, pillows and sheets off the bed, she shook them vigorously, creating a cloud of dust, then returned them to their original positions. Underneath the dust, they were fairly clean, and Mara looked forward to sleeping in comfort that night.

After urinating in the waterless toilet bowl, she returned to the living room and picked up Mary Green's letter. Maybe it would contain an explanation for this bizarre apartment. As she tore open the envelope, it suddenly occurred to Mara that this letter had been written by a woman with the same initials as her, and almost the same first name. She again wondered if this might be an illusion. Perhaps she'd gone insane. No, insane people didn't wonder if they were insane. Doubting your sanity was a sure sign you'd retained it. She placed the already opened bottle of wine on the table. Thoughts of Julie and those horrors the girl must currently be enduring again invaded Mara's head. Deciding to seek solace in alcohol, she raised the bottle to her mouth and took a long drink. She felt better almost immediately. Brushing as much dust as possible off the sofa, she removed her trainers, laid down, positioned a pillow behind her head, and examined the envelope's contents: two pages of text written in a small but neat hand.

"*February 10th, 2059.*

My Name is Mary Green. I was born in the year 2014. I grew up in the London borough of Hackney, and lived a normal childhood, or what was regarded as a normal childhood at that time. By today's standards, I suppose it would be considered rather peculiar. Sometimes, I feel as if I have fallen asleep in the world of my youth, and am now trapped in a nightmare about a totalitarian future in which society's hidden prejudices are magnified. When I was young, most people, including most politicians, believed, or claimed to believe, that women were equal to men, that homosexuals were as good as heterosexuals, that racial discrimination was a bad thing. Their commitment to equality was, of course, only a matter of fashion, as subsequent events demonstrated. But even back then, members of most minority groups - including women, who aren't a minority at all - realised how fragile their freedom was. Equality had been given them as a favour by those in a position to do so, and could just as easily be taken away again should circumstances demand it."

Mara's sense of reality was being further challenged by this text, which she might have written herself. Hadn't she said something similar to Julie just a few hours ago? The thought of Julie triggered unpleasant images Mara was determined to suppress. Taking another drink, she continued reading.

"*I had always been interested in fashion, so upon leaving university I took out a business loan and opened a shop selling women's clothing. I also created a line of designer clothes, and despite working on a small scale, I slowly but surely began building a word of mouth reputation, attracting clientele from all over the country. My business was doing well until 2045, when the government introduced a law obliging women to wear uniforms in public. This inevitably destroyed the fashion industry, and my shop had to close. As a result of my subsequent financial problems,*

I could not keep up payments on my mortgage - obtained when it was still legal for women to take out mortgages - and my house was repossessed by the bank. I soon found myself homeless, and like so many others in this situation, I gravitated towards Kilburn, which was full of abandoned property.

Choosing an apartment block at random, I found an unlocked room - Apt. 1708 - and decided to stay there. The apartment was empty, and I had brought no belongings with me, so I started scavenging, taking what I could from abandoned shops and buildings in the area. Of course, a lot of other people were doing the same thing, but when I arrived it was still easy to find good quality furniture. Whenever I came across anything valuable, which happened with remarkable frequency, I would sell it in central London, and use the money to buy food. Cooking without electricity or easy access to water was difficult, and I ended up living mostly on vegetables. I gradually filled up Apt. 1708 with found materials, and before long had it looking like a home. The inhabitants of Kilburn, perhaps disillusioned by the capitalist excesses responsible for their current state of existence, generally treated their fellow scavengers as collaborators rather than competitors, and I never had to worry about somebody walking into 'my' unlocked apartment and stealing 'my' property.

The empty houses I searched often contained clothes and books, and I could never resist taking these, even if I had no personal use for them. My neighbours quickly learned that if they wanted something to wear or something to read, I was the person to ask."

Mara felt a strange affinity for this woman she'd never met, who shared her passion for books. She put down the letter and opened another bottle of wine. She was getting very drunk. But that was good. Anything to take her mind off the torments currently being inflicted on Yuke...No, what was she thinking? Yuke was safe at home. Julie! That's who she meant. The light was starting to fade, but just enough remained for her to read the letter's final section.

"I have been living here for more than a decade, regarding my position as more or less permanent. But nothing is permanent in this world. Five days ago, the police, whom I had never so much as glimpsed in Kilburn before, turned up and started clearing out all the 'undesirables'. As I write, I am sitting at a table by the living

room window watching them arrest the occupants of a nearby apartment block. These people, many of whom I regard as friends, are being loaded into one of the three police vans parked outside the building. Yesterday, the occupants of other blocks near the one in which I reside met with the same treatment. But I intend to leave before my turn comes. Where I will go, I have no idea. But I always seem to land on my feet, and am not worried. I have discovered a spirit of community here, and I feel confident that this small flame can be fanned into a blaze which will sweep away the misogyny and injustice being foisted on this country's citizens.

I assume the police are clearing us out of Kilburn because a decision has been made to renovate the area. Perhaps this letter will end up lost amidst the debris when the contents of Apt. 1708 are thrown out. Perhaps these buildings will simply be demolished. Or perhaps nothing will be done, and a new generation of homeless will move in. If you are reading this letter, you may be one of these new homeless, in which case I wish you every happiness, and hope you make good use of what I assembled. Kilburn was a little like life to me: I brought nothing to it when I came, and I took nothing away when I left. I suggest you do the same. The only important thing is to love each other."

Mara was touched by Mary's final sentence, and pleased to find a simple explanation for this Aladdin's Cave of an apartment. But something about the letter's last paragraphs bothered her. Unfortunately, she could no longer think clearly. Her head was spinning from the wine, and she had an urge to vomit. Running into the bathroom, she threw up in the toilet bowl. Night had fallen, and what she needed now was sleep. Carefully making her way into the dark bedroom, she located the bed and groggily removed her clothes. Sleeping naked might create problems should she have to move quickly, but if a Hunter entered the apartment tonight, she'd be helpless anyway. Collapsing onto the bed, her temples throbbing, she pulled up the duvet and closed her eyes.

That night, Mara had a curious dream. She imagined herself climbing out of bed, leaving the building, and returning to the block where she had spent the previous evening. As she crossed the lobby and floated rapidly up the stairs, she was surprised to see Julie moving towards her. The girl drifted silently past. Arriving on the top floor, Mara sought out the apartment in which she'd taken refuge. She entered nervously, feeling somehow out of place, and found two women, both staring straight ahead, sitting by the wall. One of them was middle-aged, with the look of a born survivor, and although Mara had never seen Mary Green, she knew this to be her. Sitting next to Mary was Yuke. As Mara drew closer, Yuke said, "I become a different person onstage," and began singing Julie's song about the house on the edge of town.

When the song was over, Mary, still staring into the darkness, said, "That's so sad." Her voice lacked any trace of inflection or emotion.

"Yet I'm not a sad person," insisted Yuke in a similar monotone.

"Does the house represent death?" asked Mary.

"Loss of identity," responded Yuke. "Loss of individuality. Death is the ultimate loss of individuality."

Mary nodded, then said, "Are we in the house now?"

After a long pause, Yuke replied, "Not yet. Maybe soon."

Suddenly overwhelmed by the need to assert her presence, Mara shouted, "Mary, what are you doing here? You should be in your own apartment!"

Upon hearing this, Mary started laughing. Yuke turned to Mara with an expression of contempt and said, "Her name is Mara. If she tells you it's Mary, she's lying," adding, in a conspiratorial whisper, "She's full of secrets." As soon as these words were out of her mouth, a horrendous grimace appeared on Yuke's face. Pointing an accusing finger at Mara, she snarled, "But who the fuck are you?"

Mara woke up screaming. The bedroom was completely dark, and for a moment she believed herself to be in her Caledonian Road apartment. She reached over to turn on the reading light, but her hand connected only with air. When reality flooded back in and the realisation came that she was naked, unable to see anything, and in a place of great danger, her heart began racing. She felt as if she were suffocating. She took a series of long, deep breaths, trying to fight off the panic threatening to overwhelm her. After several minutes she managed to calm herself down, and eventually fell asleep again, the dream forgotten.

CHAPTER 9

Sunday March 25th

When Mara awoke the following morning, the sun appeared to have just risen. It was, she guessed, around seven a.m. Only upon sitting up did she realise how much her head ached: she had a hangover, felt sick, was dehydrated, and desperately needed water. As she climbed out of bed and pulled on her jeans - or, more accurately, Mary Green's jeans - she decided to drink an entire bottle of water. Perhaps she could make the remaining bottle last the rest of the week, along with more judicious use of the wine. She regretted getting drunk, but doing so had at least helped her stop thinking of Julie.

Mara sat on the sofa and sipped the water. Her head was clearer now, and she started rereading Mary Green's letter. She recalled being bothered by something in the final paragraphs, and thought she might be able to work out what it was now her senses were no longer quite so befuddled. The police raid was tragic, and made to seem more so by the matter-of-fact way in which it had been described, but beyond the obvious sadness of Mary's being forced to leave the apartment she'd come to regard as home, Mara still could not find anything that would explain her vague sense of disturbance. She decided to read the letter a third time. Returning to the top of page one, she glanced at the date. And then it struck her like a thunderbolt. She put the letter down and walked around the room, trying to clear her head. She kept telling herself it wasn't possible: even these people couldn't be that insane. But in her heart, she knew it was true. This letter merely confirmed something she and many others had long suspected.

The Hunt had been created in response to the bombing of the Oxford Circus tube station, a terrorist act attributed to an obscure feminist group called Backlash. Kilburn had subsequently been converted into a stadium for the Hunt. The bombing took place on February 16th, 2059, a date burned into the collective memory of an entire generation: Mara's contemporaries referred to February 16 the way their grandparents referred to September 11. But Mary's letter was dated February 10th, 2059. Why, after ignoring Kilburn for more than a decade, were the police starting to clear derelicts out of the area a week before the bombing took place? The implications were staggering: at the very least, the government must have known about the bombing in advance; most likely they were directly responsible for it. All to stir up hatred against women, and create an excuse for the Hunt. Mara remembered reading the Backlash Manifesto when it appeared online, and thinking there was something odd about it. With its dated references to 'male chauvinist pigs' and excessively strident tone, it could easily have been a misogynistic parody of feminist thought. Now everything made terrifying sense.

Mara considered the pros and cons of smuggling out the letter. There was no reason for her to be searched when leaving the arena, and even if she was, a piece of paper should be easy to conceal. But the letter didn't prove anything. The whole thing could have been a coincidence. Perhaps the London council had finally decided to renovate Kilburn - renovation had certainly been long overdue - and the government took advantage of this while looking for somewhere to stage the Hunt. There wasn't even any evidence that the letter was genuine. But Mara now knew the truth. She could not prove it, and knowing it would do her little good. But know it she did, and the knowledge struck her as strangely liberating. It was *The Wizard of Oz* in reverse: a curtain had been pulled back revealing that a supposedly benevolent ruler was actually a tyrant with undreamed of powers.

This revelation made Mara feel even more vulnerable than before. She approached the window and scanned the surrounding area. If Hunters were lurking anywhere in the vicinity, she wanted to know about it in time to take evasive action. She dimly heard church bells tolling in those parts of Kilburn situated outside the stadium walls, and wondered what worshippers made of this arena whose high walls formed such a prominent part of the landscape. How could they reconcile belief in a merciful God with the horrors being perpetrated on their doorstep? She wasn't a Christian, and the Hunters were hardly lions, but the Hunt was unquestionably a spectacle of which Nero would have approved.

Mara had been staring out the window for almost half an hour, and was about to take a break when a masculine figure wearing a backpack emerged from the door of the apartment block in which she'd spent Friday night. Mara couldn't identify the Hunter from this distance, but she suspected it was Julie's abductor who had alerted him to the presence of a potential victim in this location. She watched the man carefully as he walked towards the next building. Did he intend searching all six apartment blocks? It seemed likely. If that happened, Mara would be obliged to leave this place of relative safety, and once again take refuge in the already-searched building, at least until the Hunter departed. She kept her eyes glued to the door of the block he'd entered, waiting for him to emerge. When he reappeared almost an hour later, Mara noticed he was holding what she assumed to be a body heat detector: as Claire had suggested, it looked something like a laptop. The Hunter now approached the third apartment block. After this, there would only be one more building to go before he arrived at the block she was in.

Hurriedly pulling on the socks and trainers she'd discovered in Mary's wardrobe, Mara left the apartment, shutting the door behind her. A closed door would make the place look undisturbed should the Hunter come past, and if he assumed it was locked, he might not bother going in to scan for body heat. As she raced down the stairs, Mara thought of how rapidly this Hunter had searched the second building. He'd only taken about an hour, hardly enough time to go through every apartment, though the way he was moving from building to building suggested he was being extremely meticulous. Perhaps by merely approaching an apartment door he could detect anyone hiding in the rooms behind it.

Mara reached the ground floor in little more than ten minutes. She peered around the front door, alert for signs of activity. From this position, the grassy square obscured her view of the other doorways, so her best option was to move as rapidly as possible, hoping she didn't run headlong into a Hunter. Feeling especially glad she'd exchanged her skirt for a pair of jeans, she shot out of the building and raced towards the first block. Being outside in a place where every shadow concealed potential danger made her feel painfully exposed, and when she arrived at her destination, she tore through the entrance like a bullet, almost collapsing in the lobby. As she once again made her way through the debris, she recalled a few vague images from her dream of the previous night. Hadn't she dreamed about returning here? Perhaps her dreams were coming true. Her nightmares certainly were.

She decided to only climb up a few floors. There was no reason for the Hunter to return, and she'd be safe enough on the fifth floor while having a clear view of what was going on below. Exiting the stairwell, she walked towards those apartments that faced the building's front. All the doors were locked, so she forced open one situated in the middle of the corridor. She was astonished by how easily these flimsy structures gave way after a few hard kicks. The people who lived here must have been constantly plagued by burglars. No wonder they hadn't fought harder to prevent the banks repossessing their homes! Once inside the apartment, Mara walked over to the window and took up a position there. No more than twenty-five minutes had passed since she'd seen the Hunter enter the third block, so he'd most likely remain inside for another half hour. She patiently watched block three, and eventually saw the man emerge from the building, stand in the doorway looking around for a few seconds, and set off towards block four. She now recognised him as one of the thinner Hunters present at the initial meeting, possibly the one who'd shaken Zong's hand. And here he was two days later, still without anyone to stick needles in. Poor guy! Mara smiled as he entered the next block. She knew he'd be in there for close to an hour, so she could momentarily relax her vigilance. She decided to take a look around the apartment. It contained the usual combination of blank walls and dust. The cupboards in the kitchen were empty, and there was no water in the toilet bowl. Mara felt thirsty. Hopefully, she'd be back in what she now thought of as her apartment soon enough.

Not wanting to remain ignorant of what was going on outside, she returned to the window. Another hour passed before the Hunter came into view again. Mara thought she could see the look of disappointment and frustration on his face as he approached block five. "Get ready for some more frustration," she thought as he made his way into the building where she'd been hiding earlier that day. She wondered if he'd give up after searching this block, or if he'd explore the Leaning Tower. That construction might be habitable, but climbing from floor to floor would surely prove extremely difficult - which in itself suggested a tempting hiding place. Mara didn't dare take her eyes off the door she'd last seen the Hunter disappear through, though it seemed he'd been gone well over an hour. Was it possible he'd discovered her hiding place? Perhaps, but so what? Fascinating as the room might have been, there was nothing to suggest recent occupation. Even the uniform hung over a chair could have been there for years.

Approximately ten minutes later, Mara noticed movement in the doorway. To her dismay, it was not the Hunter who emerged, but rather Isabella, the Hunt evader who had been escorted to the stadium by two police officers. The collar locked around her throat suggested she now had an even more unpleasant escort. Mara expected to see the Hunter appear behind her, but Isabella was followed by another captive, one with waist length hair. Mara hadn't got to know this draftee on the first day of the Hunt, but she recalled that her name was Susan, and remembered thinking her hair would be a liability in the arena. As if to prove this prediction's accuracy, Susan's hair was now being gripped by the Hunter as if it were a leash. The man held a Taser in his other hand, and was pointing it at the terrified woman. He evidently only had one collar, but Susan clearly wasn't about to give him any trouble. He must be taking her back to the Hunters' block as a 'gift' for one of his fellow perverts. Was this the only communal activity these scum were capable of? Mara felt a shudder of horror. She'd now stood by helplessly as three of her comrades fell into the clutches of Hunters. She watched sadly as Isabella and Susan marched forward at the bidding of their captor. The group soon turned a corner and vanished from view.

Mara felt especially sorry for Isabella, who had been so terrified about the prospect of going on a Hunt that she'd hidden in an attic. Now she would spend the rest of the week being subjected to precisely the kind of treatment she'd so dreaded, with a lengthy prison sentence waiting for her once the ordeal ended. What especially depressed Mara was the knowledge that Isabella and Susan had been hiding in the same block as her. If she'd realised this, she could have shared her discoveries with them, and perhaps even helped them avoid capture. Or was it more likely they'd have all been caught together? These women had undoubtedly grown complacent and neglected to keep a lookout. Not that Mara was in any position to judge: she'd only noticed the Hunter by sheer chance. Leaving aside the misfortune of being conscripted, she'd had an extraordinary run of good luck. She wondered how long it would last.

Mara kept watch by the window for approximately half an hour. She didn't see any further signs of movement, and decided it was time to start making her way 'home'. As she descended the stairs and crossed the lobby, she briefly considered using the vending machine located behind the building. The chances of its having already been staked out by another Hunter were minimal, but the risk wasn't worth taking. She'd manage to survive on wine. Stepping outside, she looked about cautiously. She could run around the grassy square in little more than a minute, but the consequences of being seen during that minute were unthinkable. Fighting the impulse to remain where she was, she took a deep breath and dashed towards block five. A few yards from her destination, she tripped over some rubble, narrowly avoided falling headfirst, and propelled herself by sheer momentum through the front door. She looked back to see if anyone had followed her, but she was alone.

Ascending the stairs, Mara pondered the wisdom of remaining in what was evidently prime hunting territory. Since the Hunter was returning to his cave with not one but two prizes, it seemed reasonable to assume he'd inform his companions that these buildings had been thoroughly searched. Which probably meant Mara would be safe, or at least as safe as anywhere else in this hellish stadium. She despised herself for even thinking such things, but from a purely pragmatic perspective, every woman taken captive meant one less Hunter prowling the arena, so the longer she remained free, the less chance there was of her being discovered.

Mara soon reached the seventeenth floor, and returned to Apartment 1708, which didn't appear to have been disturbed. Hopefully, she wouldn't need to venture outside again until Friday. Here she was once more in a book-lined room she dared not leave. Home sweet home! But there were worse fates. Julie, Isabella and Susan were suffering one that very moment. Mara craved a glass of wine, but didn't want to get drunk again. She'd not eaten anything for more than twenty-four hours, but since she still felt slightly nauseous, she had no desire for food. Perhaps she'd eat half the sandwich tomorrow. In the meantime, she needed something to distract her, and books were a much better drug than alcohol. Looking through the stacks, she came across an ancient edition of Jane Austen's *Mansfield Park*. She loved Austen, but didn't feel capable of tackling her complex prose right now. A paperback of something called *The Stand* stood out by virtue of its thickness. It was by Stephen King, a writer extremely popular towards the end of the previous century. Mara had never read him before, but she was attracted by the book's sheer length - one-thousand four-hundred and twenty-one pages! If this turned out to be good, it might last her the rest of the week. She settled down on the sofa, took one drink of wine - but only one - to slake her thirst, and began reading.

King's novel proved to be excellent, and Mara was soon engrossed in this epic about a handful of people who had survived a worldwide pandemic and were making their way across a devastated American landscape. It reminded Mara of her own journey through the ruins of Kilburn. But mostly she was grateful to escape into a fictional world occupied by characters whose problems seemed, at least for a while, more important than her own. Before she knew it, she'd read almost three-hundred pages, and the light was starting to fade. Mara looked up resentfully: she did not feel in the least tired, and if a light source had been available, she'd have continued reading for hours. Using Mary's letter to mark her place, she put down the book and approached the window. The only light came from the Hunters' block. Mara shuddered as she thought of what must be going on there, of what was being done not only to Julie, but also to Susan, Isabella, and the other women who had surely been caught by now.

After drinking another glass of wine, Mara removed her clothes and climbed into bed. She wondered what Yuke was doing, and wished there was a way to let her know she'd spent most of the day reading. Yuke would have found that hilarious. As she thought of Yuke, Mara's right hand moved, almost of its own volition, until it was resting between her legs. She spent the next hour masturbating, thinking of her lover's body, imagining it there, pressing down on her. After she came, she turned on her side and slept soundly, as if safe in her own home. And that night, there were no dreams.

CHAPTER 10

Monday March 26th

Mara awoke refreshed. Her head was clear, and she looked forward to once again immersing herself in *The Stand*. Recent events had reminded her how dangerous it was to become complacent, but at the moment she seemed to be out of harm's way. A glass of wine would have to substitute for breakfast. She felt ravenously hungry, but thought it better to save the sandwich until later. Looking out the window, she noted how peaceful the area appeared. It was difficult to believe Hunters were pursuing her. Stretching out on the sofa, Mara returned to her book.

After spending five hours reading, she needed to stretch her legs. Leaving the building was out of the question, so she decided to explore the other floors. Putting on her socks and trainers, she stepped out of the apartment and strolled along the corridor. Her footsteps echoed in the silence, and she momentarily felt as if she were the last person on Earth, the final survivor of a holocaust which had wiped out all other life forms, leaving her to survive as best she could amidst the ruins of civilisation.

As she entered the stairwell, she looked over the balcony to make sure she was alone, and immediately noticed movement seven or eight floors below. A Hunter? Another woman seeking refuge? An animal? After a few seconds, the moving figure came into view, and though Mara could still not see it clearly, she recognised that glow made by the screen of a body heat detector. Mara had been prepared for something like this, and knew what course of action to take. She was obviously dealing with a Hunter going from floor to floor in search of prey. All Mara needed to do was wait until he entered a corridor. When he was out of sight, she could run down the stairs, hide on one of the lower floors he'd already searched, and remain there until he departed. Scared but confident, she peered down at the Hunter, praying he did not look up. But he was absorbed by the device in his hands. It seemed Mara's run of good luck hadn't yet been broken. Had she not decided to take a walk at that particular moment, this Hunter would certainly have caught her unawares. Mara expected him to exit the stairwell and investigate the corridor, but after staring at the detector for almost a minute, he ascended another flight of stairs. As she watched him, Mara felt fear surge through her. She now understood how the Hunter who had caught Susan and Isabella was able to search an entire building in less than an hour. Apparently, the range of these detectors wasn't as limited as she'd supposed. The Hunter merely had to stand in a stairwell, point the device at a corridor, then move up to the next level once he'd determined nobody was hiding on that floor. Which meant Mara would have no opportunity to run past him without being observed.

She felt close to fainting, but as she gripped the banister, trying to steady herself, she had an idea. The Leaning Tower was next to this building. If she could find a way of accessing the roof, she might be able to jump onto the Tower and hide there. Without a second thought, she ran up the stairs as quietly as possible. On the top floor, she found a wall-mounted frame leading to a ceiling hatchway. She climbed up and tried to unseal the hatch, which at first appeared to be locked. She pushed with all her strength, and eventually the hatch swung open. Looking back to check that the Hunter wasn't in a position to observe her, she pulled herself onto the roof. Once more, she silently thanked Mary Green for unwittingly providing her with jeans: this was another activity she'd have found it difficult to perform in a skirt. Shutting the hatch behind her, she ran across the roof and looked out at the Leaning Tower.

What she saw made her sink to her knees in anguish. The roof of the Tower was nowhere near that of the building on which she stood. Trying to leap over the gap would be suicide. Her only remaining hope was that the Hunter might end his search at the top floor, and be unable to detect her from there. She was on the side of the building furthest from the stairwell, so she still had a chance. Ten long minutes passed as she stared at the hatchway, waiting for it to be thrown open. Perhaps her luck would last a little longer.

The sight of the hatch rising and falling demonstrated in no uncertain terms that Mara's luck had finally run out. She remembered seeing Julie stand rooted to the spot in terror as a Hunter appeared before her. Now Mara knew how she felt. Her legs would not move: not that it made much difference, since there was nowhere to run. The Hunter climbed onto the roof and looked directly at her, a smile of satisfaction on his face. Mara vaguely recalled him from the meeting. He was in his forties, balding, and overweight, wearing jeans, a black leather jacket, a Dukes of Death Metal T-shirt, and a small backpack. The detector was no longer in his hands, having been replaced by a Taser.

The Hunter walked across the roof slowly but confidently, holding his Taser like a dagger. Standing in front of Mara, he took off his backpack, reached inside it, and removed a steel collar which he held out to his terrified captive. "Do you know what this is?" he asked.

Mara nodded. She wanted to speak, but the words caught in her throat. "Put it on."

Mara shook her head. "Put it on, or I'll use this," shouted the Hunter, brandishing the Taser in his other hand.

Mara managed to find her voice. "No. I'll come with you, but I won't wear a collar. Knock me out with the Taser if you like. You're the one who'll have to lower me through the hatchway and carry me down twenty floors."

The man laughed. "If I have to use the Taser, I'll lock the collar on you while you're unconscious, then wait until you wake up." Mara was forced to admit defeat. She took the collar, which looked like the rotating arm on a pair of handcuffs, only larger and thinner, with several evenly positioned holes containing electrodes on the interior. There was a ratchet at one end. Mara shuddered. She still had a slight hope of being able to run, but once she put on this collar, there would be no way to remove it without a key. The Hunter gestured with his Taser; he was becoming impatient. Mara had no choice but to place the collar around her neck and lock it into position. The click of the rotating arm engaging with the ratchet was the most hideous sound she'd ever heard.

The Hunter felt the collar to check it was secure, and with a grunt of satisfaction replaced the Taser in his backpack, which he hoisted onto his shoulders. "After you," he hissed with mock chivalry, bowing slightly as he indicated the hatchway. Mara squeezed through and descended the climbing frame, then waited in the stairwell while the Hunter followed. When he reached the bottom, he stood there staring at her, as if only just noticing she wasn't in uniform.

"Where are your clothes?" he asked.

"I left them in a room on the seventeenth floor."

"I suppose we'd better go and collect them."

As she silently walked down the stairs, the Hunter following closely behind her, Mara seemed to be looking at herself from a great distance, studying her responses as if they belonged to somebody else, clinically noting how remarkably calm she felt. But the first faint tremblings of terror were already evident, and she knew that when her mind allowed itself to acknowledge the enormity of what was happening, that terror would spread until it became the whole of her existence. The event she'd dreaded for the better part of a decade had now occurred.

When they arrived at Apartment 1708, the Hunter, suspecting a trap, insisted on entering first. He burst through the door and moved rapidly from room to room. He struck Mara as rather comical. Having satisfied himself that the apartment was empty, he beckoned for Mara to enter.

"How the fuck you find this place?" he demanded.

"I stumbled across it by accident," she replied, following him into the living room.

"You were lucky," he said, kicking a stack of books as if he found them rather loathsome. "Where's your uniform?"

"In the bedroom."

"Go get it. And be quick."

As Mara collected the uniform, her body started shaking, but she managed to control it. When she returned to the living room, the Hunter gestured at his backpack, which he'd deposited on the floor, and said, "Put 'em in there." Mara dropped her skirt, tights, blouse, jacket and shoes into the backpack, then waited while the man closed it and said, "Let's get going."

Taking one last look at the apartment where she'd hoped to spend the rest of the week quietly reading and drinking wine, Mara walked out the door. In response to a series of commands, she returned to the stairwell and began the long climb down to the ground floor. By the time they'd reached the lobby, the Hunter was visibly out of breath, and Mara felt confident she could have outrun him if she hadn't been wearing a collar. As things stood, her only option was to walk in the direction her captor indicated, towards the Hunters' block.

They made their way via a route mostly unfamiliar to Mara, but the devastation here was similar to that she'd encountered elsewhere. The Hunter walked behind Mara, ordering her to turn left here, right there. When they came to a long stretch of road which required them to walk in a straight line, the Hunter broke the silence by asking, "What's your name?"

"Mara."

"Well, well! So you're the famous Mara. We've been hearing quite a bit about you. Stop and turn around."

Mara did as she'd been told. The Hunter was holding a mobile phone, which he used to take her picture. Putting the phone back in his jacket pocket, he looked coldly at Mara and said, "I just needed some visual evidence. When the Hunt is over, I intend to report you for being out of uniform. Just a token gesture to express our appreciation for your trick with the tracking devices. Get moving."

As Mara proceeded down the road, she shouted back, "This isn't a public place, so I'm not obliged to wear a uniform."

"We'll see about that," replied the Hunter, sounding uncertain. "Go right here."

Mara turned into a relatively uncluttered street. At its end loomed the Hunters' block, a large modern structure more terrifying than any of the crumbling wrecks amidst which it was situated. Mara could not tear her eyes away from it. She didn't even perceive herself as approaching this house of torment; it was as if she were standing still while the building grew progressively larger. When she arrived at her destination, the Hunter moved in front of her and placed his thumb on a scanner attached to the door, which opened immediately. Making another mock bow, he indicated with a sweep of his arm that he required Mara to go in. She entered a well-lighted lobby with plush carpets, recently painted walls, and an elevator.

The Hunter pressed a button and the elevator doors swung open. Placing a hand on Mara's back, he gently pushed her in. They ascended swiftly to the sixth floor, where the doors automatically opened with a soft ping. "Go left," ordered the Hunter. Mara stepped out, turned left, and found herself standing in front of a door with the number eleven on it. Placing his thumb on the scanner, the Hunter opened the door and again pushed Mara in ahead of him.

The apartment's entrance hall was unexpectedly large, with several closed doors leading off it. The Hunter approached a room which, unlike the others, had an electric lock. He placed his thumb on the scanner, opened the door, and indicated that Mara should enter. To her relief, the room contained nothing, but a single bed, a wardrobe, and a window covered with bars. "This is where you'll be sleeping," said the Hunter, in what might almost have passed for a friendly voice, the voice of somebody showing a friend his guest bedroom. He pointed towards a door on the other side of the room.

"That's the bathroom. You'll find a robe in there. You've got half an hour to take a shower, change into the robe, and have a short rest. After that, I'll give you something to eat, and we can have a chat in the living room."

He walked quietly out of the bedroom, shutting the door behind him. Mara waited a few seconds, then tried to open it. She wasn't exactly surprised to discover it had been locked.

Mara's head started spinning. What kind of 'chat' were they going to have? And what would happen after the 'chat'? There was no point kidding herself. She knew perfectly well what she'd been brought here for. She sat on the edge of the bed and clenched her hands into fists, squeezing so tightly her nails dug into the flesh of her palms, trying to suppress the panic rising in her throat. She began moaning softly, like a trapped animal, but quickly checked herself. If she was going to survive the next few days with her sanity intact, she'd need every ounce of self-control she could muster. She entered the bathroom, noticing a long black silk robe hanging by the door. Hot water issued from the shower at the touch of a button. Mara removed what she was wearing and stepped into the stall. It felt good to wash off the accumulated dirt of the last few days. She found a bar of soap and a bottle of shampoo, and used the latter to wash her hair. A large towel had been placed on the bathroom cabinet; Mara wrapped it around her. The cabinet contained a toothbrush, toothpaste, a hairbrush, more soap, a plastic cup, bandages, and even sanitary towels. Somebody had thought of everything! She brushed her teeth, turning on the tap by the sink as she did so. The sight of running liquid seemed almost miraculous, and she used the cup to take several drinks of cold water.

When she'd finished, Mara placed her clothes in the wardrobe - even hangers had been provided! - sat on the bed, and dried her hair with the towel, using the brush to comb it. She might as well look good for her torturer! She slipped into the robe, tying the sash around her waist. Peering through the bars on the window, she could see the apartment block where she'd spent Friday night. She recalled standing inside it, looking at the Hunters' building in the distance. And now, here she was, returning the look. She laid on the bed, closed her eyes, and waited for the Hunter to return. She'd never been so scared, but at the same time she experienced a sense of resignation. The worst had happened, and the curse of uncertainty lifted.

Mara soon heard the bedroom door opening. The Hunter stood there, smiling at her. "You look nice," he said. "Follow me."

He led her into the living room. It contained a sofa next to a table on which sat a plate of baked beans, some toast, and a cup of coffee. Despite not having eaten for days, Mara couldn't stomach much in the way of food, but the hot coffee was welcome, and she managed to swallow a slice of toast. As she did this, the Hunter sat beside her and said, "First things first. My name is Stephen Tyner. I completely understand that you don't want to be here, and I know we got off on the wrong foot. But the situation is what it is. There's nothing you can do to change it, so I suggest you make the best it. Our real work won't begin until tomorrow, but after we've finished talking, we'll have a short session in the playroom. Just enough to give you some idea what'll be expected of you." He paused as if waiting for a response, but Mara only stared at him, her eyes wide with dread. His calmly reasonable manner was intimidating her more than a display of overt sadism would have done. "Is there anything you'd like to know?" he asked.

Trying to suppress her fear, Mara said, "I spent Friday night with a woman called Julie. She was caught on Saturday morning. She's extremely vulnerable, and I'd like to know if she's okay."

"I'll ask around and see if I can find out how she's doing, though you might need to rethink what you mean by 'okay'. I assume you're aware of what goes on here."

Mara nodded.

"And how do you feel about it?" asked Tyner.

Mara thought for a moment before replying. "I'm more scared than I've ever been in my life."

Tyner seemed inexplicably pleased with this answer, and slapped his knee in satisfaction. "Well," he said, "I can assure you I know exactly what I'm doing. I'm not saying a word against the other Hunters - we get together to compare notes most evenings, and they're a great bunch of guys - but I have a feeling they're pretty new to this kind of thing."

"You mean rape and torture?" responded Mara with a forthrightness that surprised even her.

Tyner smiled understandingly. "Let me tell you something about myself. I probably wouldn't be sitting here today if it hadn't been for a book. Anyone who knows me would be surprised to hear that. I've never made any secret of the fact I hate books. I was forced to read them in school, and loathed every minute. It seemed obvious to me that writers were afraid of life. They made up stories about people who did things because they were incapable of doing things themselves. And of course, everyone who doesn't want to live in the real world loves reading. It's so much easier than dealing with reality. It's mostly girls and queers who read a lot anyway."

Mara was almost tempted to point out that she fell into both these categories, but decided it would be better to let this pathetic creep speak without interruption.

"I only read one book after leaving school. It was called *Fifty Shades of Grey*. My sister had it, and I happened to pick it up while visiting her. I didn't read the whole thing - I don't have that kind of time to waste - but I skimmed it, and it was a real eye-opener. According to this book, women want to be dominated by men, and are turned on sexually when men tie them up, or punish them in some way. It's called a BDSM relationship. This woman who's like the central character, she falls in love with a man because he does these things to her."

Mara had to interrupt at this point. "Some women like that, but some don't. Most don't. I have absolutely no desire to be tied up or beaten."

Tyner suddenly became impassioned. "That's where you're wrong. You want to be dominated. You just don't know it. The woman in this book, at first she was terrified at the idea of BDSM, but once she'd experienced it, she loved it. It turned her on when she was given, like, punishment."

Mara shook her head. "I was given a judicial caning once, and I can assure you I didn't find it erotic."

Tyner leaned forward, obviously interested by this.

"Ah, so you've already had some experience."

Mara tried to conceal her frustration. "I'm not sure what you mean by 'experience'. I broke the law, and was punished. The punishment was definitely not intended to turn me on."

"What were you punished for?"

"Being out of uniform in a public place."

"You seem to make a habit of that."

"I already told you, the arena isn't a public place. Anyway, if you hadn't forced me to leave, I'd have stayed in the apartment."

"Anyway, tell me about your caning."

Mara had no wish to discuss this subject, but she was willing to grasp at anything that might delay her 'session' in the playroom.

"I went out to do some shopping without getting changed first. A police officer scanned my thumbprint, and when he found I was over eighteen, he said I'd be hearing from the authorities. Three days later, I received a letter saying I had to report to a punishment centre."

"How did you feel when you read the letter?"

"Awful. I thought of appealing, but I didn't have grounds for an appeal."

"What happened when you went to the centre? Tell me everything you remember."

"I handed the letter to a receptionist, and was told to sit in the waiting area. Eventually, two women came and escorted me to a room. It was empty except for a padded flogging bench. One of the women ordered me to remove everything except my blouse and lie face down on the bench. Once

I was in position, they strapped me down so I couldn't move. The first woman said, 'Mara Gorki, you have been sentenced to ten strokes of the cane for violating uniform regulations. The punishment will be carried out immediately.' I think those were her exact words. Then she began beating me. The other woman counted out each stroke. I thought it would never end, but I guess the caning only took about three minutes. After the last stroke, the woman undid the straps and said, 'You may get dressed and leave when you are ready.'"

"Did the cane draw blood?" asked Tyner, almost breathlessly.

Mara lowered her head, causing strands of hair to fall forwards and cover her eyes. With surprising gentleness, Tyner brushed these strands back, caressing her cheek lightly as he did so. Mara looked up, a tear rolling down her face, and nodded. She wanted to lie, but felt almost hypnotised by this brute. Neither of them had to spell out what was implied by Tyner's question and her response; that blood would soon be drawn once more. Suddenly, Tyner lunged forward and licked away the tear. Mara gasped as she smelled his rancid breath. "Go on," Tyner whispered in her ear.

"I... I couldn't sit down afterwards," Mara stuttered, pulling away from her tormentor, "and the bruises... the bruises were still visible a week later. It was one of the most unpleasant experiences of my life."

"I think you're being dishonest," said Tyner as he settled back in his chair. "I guarantee that at some level you were turned on, and you're, like, afraid to admit it. Over the next few days, you're going to learn a few things about yourself that will surprise you. The fact you've absolutely no choice is precisely what will make this experience such an exciting one. I've spent a lot of money paying prostitutes for BDSM sessions, and what always spoils it is their insistence on having, like, a safe word. That's why I was willing to pay far more to take part in a Hunt. This way, I get to play with someone who has no safe word, no control over what happens. Of course, there are limits set by the Hunt committee, but they're not set by you."

"But BDSM is by definition consensual. If you remove the element of consent, you can't call it BDSM."

Tyner looked thoughtful. "Maybe you're right. Maybe I should use another word."

Mara felt like screaming, but she managed to control her voice.

"I know the word you should use. Torture! That's what you're planning to do to me! At least call it what it is!"

"Torture is used to get, like, information or a confession. The person being tortured knows their ordeal will end once they do what the torturer wants. That's not what's going to happen here. There's no information you can give, no confession you can make, that will stop the pain. This is about exploring your limits. You should see me as a guide."

Mara could take no more. She screamed and put her hands over her ears, trying to shut out this lunacy. Tyner was not disturbed by this: indeed, it seemed to have been what he was waiting for. He calmly picked up a tissue, used it to dry the tears pouring down Mara's face, and put his arm around her shoulders in a comforting manner as he said, "Mara, you have to be strong now. We're going to move into the playroom."

He stood up, took her hands, and gently urged her to her feet. As if in a trance, Mara allowed herself to be led out to the hallway. Positioning her before one of the closed doors, Tyner stroked her hair with something which might have passed for affection and asked, "Are you ready?"

Mara shook her head and looked at him beseechingly, her eyes again full of tears.

"No, please. I don't want to do this."

Tyner caressed her cheek.

"I think you're ready, Mara. I think you're much stronger than you suspect."

Saying this, he opened the door and pushed her in. At first, the room was completely dark. Tyner reached for a switch and turned on the lights with one hand, shutting the door behind him with the other.

For some reason, the first thing Mara noticed was that the room had no windows. It was a small point, but it clearly defined this as a space set apart from the everyday world, a space from which there was no hope of rescue, nothing to intervene between victim and torturer. Mara took in the room's contents instantly, as if the image had been imprinted on her retinas by a flash of lightning. There was a padded flogging bench, a large X-shaped cross standing upright by a wall, ropes hanging from bars attached to the ceiling, and a wooden horse, shaped like an upside down V, with restraints to hold its rider in place. Arranged on shelves around the room were vibrators, handcuffs, ball gags, whips, canes, clamps, and an electrical device to which long wires were attached. Mara was in no doubt as to the purpose of all this equipment. It was to be used on her body, used to restrain her, humiliate her, and above all cause her pain. Tyner observed her response carefully, and chose the moment when an expression of total horror had spread across her face to say, in a soft voice, "Mara, I want you to take off your robe and hand it to me."

Mara shook her head. The thought of being naked in this place was more than she could stand. Tyner spoke more forcefully this time. "All we're going to do today is have a one-hour session. But if you don't take off your robe by the time I count to five, I'll double the session's length." He started counting, but Mara had already removed her robe by the time he reached two. Taking the garment and hanging it on a hook by the door, Tyner turned to the terrified and naked Mara, gestured at the X-shaped cross in the corner of the room, and said, "Walk over to that cross and stand with your back to it." Mara did as she'd been ordered, shuddering at the feel of the cross's cold wooden surface. Tyner raised her left arm above her head, lining it up with the restraint on the cross's top left corner. Once it was in position, he tightly secured the strap around her wrist, then lifted her right arm to the top right corner and secured it in the same way. Bending down, he said, "Spread your legs as wide as you can," and proceeded to fasten the straps attached to the bottom left and right corners of the cross around her ankles. By the time he'd finished, Mara could not move an inch. Tyner walked across the room, and as soon as he'd vacated the space in front of her, Mara noticed a full-length mirror positioned directly opposite the cross. The sight of herself in this humiliating position added to her terror, as it was plainly intended to do.

Opening a white box sitting on one of the shelves, Tyner removed a small object which Mara could not make out. As he moved closer, she saw it was a medical needle in a sterile wrapper. "No!" she sobbed. "Please, not that!"

Tyner smiled as he unwrapped the needle.

"You don't even know what I'm going to do with this yet."

Mara stared at the needle, breathing heavily. Tyner pushed a lock of hair out of her face.

"I need you to listen carefully. Can you do that, Mara?"

Mara nodded, her fear growing with every moment. "That's good," said Tyner. "In a moment, I'm going to pierce your left nipple with this needle."

Mara finally lost control. "No!" she screamed. "Please, don't. I beg you. I can't take it!"

"Mara..." said Tyner, as if talking to an unreasonable child, but Mara did not let him finish.

"You don't understand, I really can't take this."

She pulled desperately at her restraints. Tyner stroked her face as he said, "When I pierce your left nipple, I want you to describe what it feels like. It's important you be completely honest. If I suspect you're lying or concealing anything, I'll take another needle and pierce your right nipple. Do you understand?"

Mara stared at Tyner unbelievingly, but it was obvious nothing she said would deter him. "J...just tell you what it f...feels like?" she stuttered. Tyner nodded.

"That's all you have to do."

He grabbed Mara's left breast, squeezed the nipple between two of his fingers, and pressed the needle against it, saying, "I'm going to pierce you now." Mara screamed as the needle worked its way in.

"What does it feel like?"

"It hurts, it hurts so much. Please, stop."

"Okay, it hurts, but how exactly does it make you feel?" asked Tyner as he pushed the needle deeper.

"It...it makes me feel helpless. You're causing me so much pain for no reason. I c...can't move. All I can do is watch as you d...do this to me. Oh God!"

Mara's final exclamation coincided with the moment when the needle's tip emerged from the opposite side of her nipple. Tyner stepped back, leaving the needle in place, and Mara saw a thin line of blood run down her breast.

"That was very good, Mara. Now I've one more question to ask, and I want you to think for a minute before saying anything, because your answer must be completely truthful. Were you at all turned on by what I just did?"

Mara took a deep breath. The pain was intolerable, and she desperately wanted the needle removed. But she doubted this lunatic would accept the truth, which is that she found what he was doing to her painful and humiliating, not erotic. She knew what he wanted to hear, and after waiting a minute, she said, in a voice she tried to make as convincing as possible, "It was horrible, but I have to admit I was excited by it."

Tyner reached down and felt between Mara's legs, probing her vagina with his index finger. Removing his hand, he held it up in front of him and said, in an disappointed tone, "Completely dry. I'm afraid you were lying. That means you get the second needle."

He turned away and returned to the white box as Mara screamed. "You lied to me," hissed Tyner as he unwrapped another needle, "and I told you what would happen if you lied."

"You won't accept the truth. You think I'm going to be turned on, but I'm not. You can't imagine how painful this is. It's horrific. I don't want this. Don't you understand? I don't want this!"

Tyner was already holding Mara's right breast, once again positioning the nipple between his fingers.

"You don't have to say anything this time. Just focus on the pain."

As before, Tyner placed the needle on the nipple's edge and, after holding it there for a few seconds as he stared into Mara's face, began pushing it in. Mara cried out and pulled at her restraints, but the needle continued to make its slow progress, and Tyner was soon standing back admiring his handiwork. Mara looked down helplessly as a second line of blood appeared. Tyner nodded, evidently satisfied with a job well done, then glanced at his watch and said, "I promised you this first session would only last an hour, and there's still twenty-five minutes to go, so I'm going to leave you on the cross for the remaining time while I take care of a few other things. When I come back, I'll let you down, and you can go to bed."

"Please, take the needles out!" Mara implored. But Tyner had already shut the door behind him. Mara was left confronting her own reflection in the mirror. The sight of herself with needles in each nipple and blood running down her breasts was unbearable, and she shut her eyes tightly, trying to ignore the throbbing pain. After what seemed an eternity, the door opened again and Tyner re-entered. Taking some disinfectant and cotton wool from a medical box, he removed the needles, threw them into a nearby basket, and gently wiped Mara's breasts, meticulously cleaning off the blood. When he'd finished, he undid the restraints on her ankles and wrists. She almost collapsed when her hands were freed, and Tyner had to support her as she returned to the bedroom.

"You did well this evening," he remarked as she fell onto the bed. "Now try to get some sleep. Tomorrow is going to be a long day." He shut the door quietly.

As she lay there in the dark, Mara's despair was devastating. She'd fallen into the clutches of a psychopath to whom there could be no appeal for mercy. She experienced a terror so overwhelming her conscious mind could not accommodate it, and almost immediately fell into a deep sleep which was more like a trance, or even a descent into madness. Mara dreamed she was back on the train, being abused by those sadistic young men. When she looked up at the ringleader, she saw Tyner standing there shouting, "Banooseferoo! Banooseferoo!" as he tore pages from her copy of *The Aging Boy* and threw them in her face.

CHAPTER 11

Tuesday March 27th

Mara awoke with a start as light penetrated the window. There was no clock in her room, but she guessed it to be six or seven in the morning. Her breasts were still sore, though the throbbing pain had finally subsided. Reaching up to touch her neck, she was surprised to find it enclosed in a steel band. She'd completely forgotten about the collar. She stared at the locked door. Her captor could come through it at any moment and begin subjecting her to more torment. Tyner obviously saw her as a kind of doll he could play with as long as he wanted, twisting its head off or throwing it against a wall if the mood struck him. She had to make him see her as a human being.

She used the toilet and brushed her teeth, then drank two cups of water. The clothes she'd hung in the wardrobe had vanished. Tyner must have taken them while she was hanging from the cross. Or perhaps he came into the room while she was sleeping. There was certainly nothing to prevent him doing so. As far as she knew, her uniform was still in his backpack, and the robe had been left in the playroom. She took the bathroom towel and wrapped it around her. Then she sat on the bed and waited.

Hours seemed to pass before Mara heard a faint click and saw the door swing open. Tyner was standing there, her robe in his hand. "Good morning," he said cheerfully. "You forgot this last night." He handed her the robe, which she took without saying a word. "Get dressed. I've made you some breakfast."

"Where are my clothes?"

"If you're referring to the clothes you shouldn't have been wearing, I've thrown them away. If you're referring to the clothes you should have been wearing, I've put them in the washing machine, along with your underwear. They'll be ready by Friday. Until then, the robe is all you'll need."

Tyner held the door open and waited as Mara removed her towel and put on the robe. Then she followed him into the kitchen, where toast and coffee were waiting. Mara sat at the table and tried eating the toast. She still didn't feel hungry, but knew it was important to keep up her strength. The coffee tasted good, and when Tyner offered her a second cup, she accepted. "Well," he said, sitting down opposite her, "How do you feel about last night?"

Mara considered her words carefully. "Look, I understand your viewpoint. But I think it must be obvious to both of us that I don't want this. Even you had to admit I wasn't turned on by what you did yesterday. I realise you've paid a lot of money for the right to do this. Maybe I could find a way to pay you back."

Tyner shook his head. "It's not about money, Mara. You know that. It's about testing your limitations."

Mara tried to remain calm. "But I don't want my limitations tested. I really don't. I haven't just...just...I...I don't exist so you can...can satisfy your desires. I have a life. I have friends. I have people who love me, people who are worried sick about what's happening to me right now. I'm...I'm a creative person. I know you don't think much of writers, but I'm a novelist. Maybe you're right when you say people like me are afraid of the real world, but if the real world is anything like your playroom, you can't blame me for being afraid of it. Please, just let me go back to my little world."

"You will go back to your little world, Mara. Only when you do, you'll be much stronger. I get where you're coming from. I wouldn't have said those things about writers if I'd, like, known you were one. But this experience will make you a better artist. And I know what I'm talking about. I'm an artist myself. I design video games."

Mara couldn't help laughing, though she immediately regretted doing so. "What's funny about that?" demanded Tyner.

Mara tried to change the expression on her face. "Nothing, really nothing. It's just that after all those things you said about people writing books because they're afraid of living real lives, I...I just...I'm a little surprised to hear..."

For the first time, Tyner seemed genuinely angry. "Video games are the most important art-form of the century. Do you actually know anything at all about them? Do you realise how much work goes into making one? No, you obviously don't. But that doesn't stop you assuming you're fucking superior to people who have the skill to...to..."

Mara took hold of Tyner's hand and tried to calm him down. "I'm sorry. I'm genuinely sorry. I shouldn't have laughed. I don't think I'm superior to you. But I do know a little about video games, and...Stephen, I...Life isn't like a video game. When you get killed in real life, you don't jump up and start again. I'm a woman. A real woman. I'm not a collection of pixels. When you stick needles in me, I feel pain." She drew aside her robe to show him her breasts. "Look. You can see the bruises on my nipples. They still hurt. Let's stop this. Maybe you could tell me about video games. I'm terribly ignorant. You could educate me. I'd be really interested."

Tyner smiled. "I shouldn't have lost my temper with you, Mara. I know it's not your fault. And I do appreciate that you're under a lot of pressure. If you'd like to discuss video games, look me up once the Hunt is over and I'll be happy to tell you all about them. But right now, it's time for us to spend out first full day in the playroom."

He stood up and held out his hand. Tears appeared on Mara's cheeks. She saw this was inevitable. Placing her hand in Tyner's, she let herself be led to the playroom. Tyner opened the door and walked in, turning on the light as he did so, and Mara followed without having to be urged. After closing the door, Tyner removed Mara's robe. She allowed it to be taken without protesting.

Tyner approached a bench in the middle of the room. It consisted of a wooden frame with padding on top and straps designed to hold its victim in a bending position. He looked at Mara, standing naked near the door, and said, "This is a flogging bench. How does it compare with the one on which you received your judicial caning?"

Mara apprehensively approached the device and said, "The...the one in the punishment centre was completely flat. Not like this at all."

"Bend over this one," ordered Tyner. Mara was too terrified to resist. Tyner placed her wrists in the restraints, then secured her ankles. He selected a cane from one of the shelves.

"Does this look like the cane that was used on you?"

Mara stared at the cane, a tear running down her face. "I guess so. I didn't see it that clearly."

Tyner stood behind Mara, lined up the cane, and brought it down on her buttocks. Mara let out a scream.

"Was that harder, softer, or about the same as the strokes you received?"

Mara hardly knew what to say. "I...I think it was about the same."

"Excellent. And when did this caning take place?"

"A...about six years ago."

"So if you could take ten strokes then, you should easily be able to withstand fifty now."

"Oh no, please!"

"And I'm growing tired of your begging. So here's a new rule. You may scream all you want, but every time you say 'no', or 'please' or 'don't', or anything like that, I'll add another five strokes to the total. Do you understand?"

Mara nodded, and Tyner began beating her, leaving a few seconds between each stroke: she inadvertently shouted "No!" at one point, and ended up receiving fifty-five.

The rest of the day passed in much the same fashion. Donning a pair of surgical gloves, Tyner inserted first three fingers, then a vibrator, and finally a large dildo into Mara's anus. He beat her again, this time with a wooden paddle. After releasing her from the flogging bench, he returned her to the X-shaped cross, securing her so she was facing away from him, and flogged her with a thick whip until her back was raw, then turned her around and beat her breasts with a leather strap: he initially announced he would give her twenty strokes, but when Mara complained her nipples were still sore from yesterday's treatment, he doubled the amount to forty. Mara didn't say anything after that. He whipped her stomach and the front of her thighs with a riding crop, attached a paper clamp to her clitoris, and walked out of the room, leaving her to stare at the reflection of her bruised body in the mirror.

An hour later, the door opened and Tyner reappeared, accompanied by an elderly bearded man. "Here's the patient," Tyner cheerfully announced as he gestured at Mara.

The stranger didn't seem surprised at Mara's condition, simply saying, "Let's get her down and take a look at her." While Tyner removed the clamp and started to undo the ankle straps, the stranger addressed Mara. "Miss Gorki, I'm Dr. Roberts. I'm here to see how you're getting on. Once we have you down from here, we'll go into the bedroom and I'll examine you."

As Tyner undid the wrist straps, he asked Dr. Roberts, "Could you check her to see if she can take electricity?"

"No problem," replied the doctor.

Mara was unable to stand, so Tyner and the doctor carried her out and laid her on the bed. Mara was surprised to find it was already night. After Tyner had left the room, Dr. Roberts opened his medical bag and said, "How are you feeling, Miss Gorki?"

The question struck Mara as so ridiculous that she burst out crying. "Look at me!" she sobbed. "Just look at me!"

The doctor asked Mara to roll onto her front, and as he cleaned her wounds asked, "Has Mr. Tyner been doing anything he's not supposed to?"

Mara could hardly get the words out. "He...he pierced my nipples with needles. He put a clamp...down there...beat me all over...he.."

The doctor interrupted. "These are all approved activities. Has he done anything you believe may not be approved?"

And insane as it sounded, Mara had to admit he hadn't. Dr. Roberts removed a blood pressure monitor from his bag, attached it to her upper arm, and made a note of the reading, then used a stethoscope to check her heartbeat. "All fine," he declared, and tried to open the door. Finding it locked, he shouted impatiently. Tyner quickly appeared.

"Sorry, I hadn't realised I'd shut it all the way. It locks automatically."

"I'm aware of that," said the doctor. "I'm satisfied with our patient's condition, but I think she should rest until tomorrow morning. Try to avoid hitting her buttocks again. But you have my permission to use electricity. Let's go in the other room and I'll write you an official slip."

The men departed, closing the door behind them. Mara stared into space. Eventually, the door opened again and Tyner came back in.

"Looks like I was a little hard on your rear. Sorry about that. I'll make you some supper."

He returned an hour later, handed Mara her robe, and asked her to join him in the living room. She found a large pizza and a bottle of wine on the table, along with two plates and two glasses. The pizza evoked memories of her weekends with Yuke, memories that were unwelcome in this context, and eating it was like trying to eat cardboard. The wine she drank gratefully, and quickly consumed three glasses, hoping to find the oblivion she craved. As she reached for the bottle to pour a fourth glass, Tyner took it out of her hand, saying, "I think you've had enough wine. We need to make sure you have a clear head tomorrow. Tell me what you made of today's session."

Mara stared at him with contempt, then stood up and lifted her robe so he could see the bruises and welts covering her body. "What do you think I made of today's session?" she asked.

Tyner pulled a face which suggested she was being unreasonable. "You're experiencing something new here. I wouldn't expect you to appreciate it right away. But wait and see what you feel like by the end of the week."

Mara turned towards him angrily. "You keep talking about what *I* have to experience, about testing *my* limitations. What about *your* limitations? Has anyone ever tested how much pain *you* can endure? Wouldn't it be fair for us to reverse positions? Why don't I beat you tomorrow?"

Tyner smiled as if he were humouring a child. "Mara, Mara. I'm sure you don't need me to tell you that men who like being dominated are queers. The fact is, it's natural for men to dominate women. Nature decided this by making us physically stronger than you. This is why women like it when men behave aggressively, why they're turned on when men punish them. You don't think you're turned on because decades of feminazi brainwashing have convinced you women are equal to men. Thank God we now have a new society in which the damage is being undone. You're still thinking the old way, but soon your body will learn the lesson I'm teaching it."

Mara remembered Mary Green's letter. She knew geeks loved conspiracy theories. Perhaps letting Tyner know what she'd discovered would make him feel a kinship with her. "Let me tell you something about your new society," she began. "In the apartment where I was hiding, I found a letter written by a woman who'd been living there. According to her, the police started clearing all the homeless out of Kilburn one week before the 2059 bombings. You see what that means? The government must have known about the bombings, or even been responsible for them. All to provide an excuse for the Hunt."

Tyner looked mildly amused. "I'm not even going to bother telling you how crazy that sounds, Mara. Now the doctor has suggested you could do with an evening off, and after listening to your paranoid rant, I'm inclined to agree with him. What would you like to do? We could watch some television."

Mara looked down at the pizza. "Could I just be on my own now?" she asked quietly.

Tyner was obviously disappointed. "Fine. If you don't like my company you may go to your room."

Mara walked out without saying another word, and Tyner followed her. After opening the bedroom door, he said, "Have a good night's sleep. I'll see you tomorrow morning," and left her alone in the darkness. Removing her robe, she climbed onto the bed and attempted to find a comfortable position. Lying on her back proved too painful, so she tried resting on her side. There was a ceiling-mounted light, but with nothing to read, there wasn't any point turning it on. As Mara stared into emptiness, heavy metal began playing loudly in the living room. She'd always hated heavy metal, and thought it somehow appropriate that a man like Tyner would be into this kind of thing. The throbbing beat shook the walls, recalling the relentless fury with which Tyner had struck her. She could almost feel his anger. Mara supposed she should be grateful Tyner hadn't played something she liked. Hearing Mozart or Leonard Cohen or Billie Holiday under these circumstances would have tainted them irretrievably for her, though she doubted anyone who listened to Billie Holiday would have been quite so eager to torture women. She'd heard of concentration camp commandants relaxing by playing Schubert on the piano. Did that really happen, or was it a myth? She found it much easier to imagine fascists listening to that celebration of raw brutality issuing from the next room. Tyner had turned the volume up as high as possible, preventing Mara from sleeping. As she lay there, memories of the things which had been done to her that day, alongside thoughts of the things that would be done to her tomorrow, came crashing in. She tried to fight them off by focusing on the mental image of a blank wall. Eventually, Tyner turned the music down. Mara spent the few hours of sleep available to her dreaming of a familiar voice demanding that she wake up.

CHAPTER 12

Wednesday March 28th

The sound of the door opening jolted Mara awake. The first thing she saw was Tyner entering the room, a smile on his face.

"I'll give you half an hour to pull yourself together. Then we can have breakfast."

He shut the door without waiting for a response. Mara sat up in bed, pushing the hair out of her eyes. She knew what this madman was planning for today, had heard him discuss it with the doctor. She stumbled towards the bathroom, urinated and brushed her teeth, then took a shower. It did not leave her feeling refreshed. Pulling on her robe, she sat on the edge of the bed, her anguish growing with every moment. Burying her head in her hands, she began to sob. Tyner discovered her in this position. Ignoring her distress, he barked, "Let's go!" and held the door open.

Mara walked into the living room, where a mug of coffee awaited her. Tyner sat next to her on the sofa and said, "I've only made you coffee this morning, because we're going to do something involving the use of a ball gag, and I don't want you vomiting while you have it on."

"Great," replied Mara as she drank the coffee.

Ignoring her sardonic tone, Tyner continued. "I'm very pleased with the work we've done so far, but today I want to take things onto, like, another level. I assume you have some idea what's going to happen. Before you start complaining, read this."

He passed her a printed form on which names and dates had been written in the blank spaces provided.

"This is to certify that <u>Mara Gorki</u> was examined by <u>Dr. Alex Roberts</u> on <u>March 27th, 2068</u>, and is deemed fit to withstand electric shock treatment as part of the Hunt commencing <u>March 23rd</u> and ending <u>March 30th</u>. Signed: <u>Dr. Alex Roberts</u>."

"This is insanity," observed Mara to herself as Tyner took the letter and placed it in his pocket.

"Now I know you like to claim you can't take the things I do to you in the playroom, but this time you've been examined by a doctor and certified fit to receive electric shocks. So do you agree with this medical professional that you can take electric shock treatment, or do you want to offer, like, an amateur opinion on the subject?"

Mara looked at him and said, "Don't worry. I know there's no point arguing with you. I used to think you didn't see me as a human being. But that wasn't the problem at all. The problem is that you aren't a human being. You're...I don't know what you are. Even an animal wouldn't behave this way. You...you..."

Mara was barely able to breathe, and Tyner stroked her face, saying, "Calm down, calm down." He didn't seem angry.

When Mara began breathing more normally, Tyner suggested she use the bathroom. "Electric shocks can cause loss of bowel and bladder control, so it's best you be as empty as possible." He escorted her back to the bedroom and said, "I'll give you twenty minutes."

Mara found she actually did need to have a bowel movement, her first since the Hunt began. When Tyner returned, she was sitting on the bed waiting.

As soon as they entered the Playroom, Tyner told Mara to take off her robe, and moved her gently but firmly towards a padded bench which looked like a gynaecological examination chair. Knowing she had no choice, Mara sat in the chair and placed her legs in the stirrups. Tyner fastened restraints around her ankles and thighs, then walked to the chair's rear, commanding Mara to lean forward and open her mouth. As she did this, a red ball gag was forced between her teeth. Tyner tightly secured the gag's strap, explaining, "This is mainly to prevent you biting your tongue. The fact that it stops you nagging is just a bonus." He smiled at her, as if this were their private joke. After securing restraints around Mara's stomach, arms and neck, he went to a nearby table and picked up an electrical generator. Wires ending in alligator clips were connected to it. Tyner untangled the wires and attached one of the clips to Mara's left toe. After checking the generator's settings, he pressed a button. Mara felt electricity surge through her body. She tried to scream, but could not. Tyner shocked her four more times, relishing the way she struggled futilely against the restraints, then removed the clip, fastened it on her left nipple, and delivered another five shocks. To finish up, he attached the clip to her clitoris. By the time he removed the ball gag, she was unable to speak. Tyner used a tissue to wipe her mouth, and said, "Now rest for a few minutes while I prepare your next challenge."

Mara watched helplessly as Tyner laid a mat on the floor by the wooden horse, and tugged on some ropes hanging from the ceiling. He left the room, and came back a few minutes later with a glass of water, which he allowed Mara to drink, holding her head and slowly pouring the liquid into her mouth. When the glass was empty, he removed Mara's restraints and helped her climb off the chair. She had trouble standing, and almost collapsed. "You seem a little unsteady," observed Tyner. "But don't worry. What's coming next will enable you to take the weight off your feet. Lie face down on the mat."

Once Mara was in position, Tyner ordered her to place her hands behind her back. Using a length of thick string, he bound Mara's wrists, then began tying a rope suspended from the ceiling under her arms. When he'd finished, he tugged on the other end of the rope, pulling Mara into the air, and slowly lowered her onto the wooden horse. Mara was now straddling the upside down V, and as the full weight of her body pressed down on the wood's sharp edge, she began sobbing. Tyner secured Mara's legs tightly in the restraints attached to either side of the horse, then left the room. As with the cross, a mirror had been positioned before this device so its victim could observe herself. Mara tried shifting position, but the limited amount of movement permitted by the restraints meant that all she succeeded in doing was spreading the pain to a slightly different area.

Mara had no idea how long she'd been on the horse. Time had ceased to have any meaning. She now inhabited an eternity of suffering in which each moment was as unendurable as the last. When the door again opened, she could not have said if she'd been on the horse for an hour or a day. Tyner entered, Dr. Roberts close behind him. The doctor took one look at her and said, "Let's get Miss Gorki down from there so I can examine her."

Mara almost wept tears of joy. She could not have endured another minute of this. Tyner was plainly frustrated. "She's almost at the mid-point of an eight-hour session, and I'd hate to break it. Can't you examine her where she is?"

The doctor frowned, but said, "I guess it'd be okay."

As Tyner left the room, Mara began pleading with Dr. Roberts. "Doctor, I can't take any more of this. I beg you, please let me down."

The doctor was examining Mara's body with apparent professional disinterest. Taking a stethoscope from his medical bag, he reached up and checked her heartbeat, observing, "Your heart is beating quite steadily, all things considered. I see no reason to intervene. I realise this is extremely painful. It's undoubtedly designed to be. But I guarantee it won't cause any permanent damage. After you've been up there five or six hours, the pain starts to diminish and numbness sets in, so it won't be as bad as you think. Was there anything you wanted to report?"

Mara stared down at him in disbelief. "Look at me!" she screamed. "Look what's being done to me! How the fuck can you allow this? What kind of doctor are you?"

Roberts seemed genuinely offended. "I can assure you I am doing the job assigned me to the best of my ability. If I were to say you are not capable of enduring another four hours on the horse, I would be lying. Do you wish me to lie?"

"Yes, doctor. I wish you to lie. I wish you to lie, because under the present circumstances that would be the only sane course of action you could take."

Snapping his bag shut, the doctor stormed out without saying another word. Mara expected Tyner to return immediately, but it soon became obvious she wouldn't see him again until the time came for her to be taken down. She could no longer even pretend to understand what motivated him. If he derived a sadistic thrill from seeing her in agony, why didn't he stay to watch? Tyner reminded her of the merciless but also emotionless torturers in Pasolini's *Salo*, incapable of even taking a perverse pleasure from their sadistic activities. He was like an alien life form, motivated by desires and impulses impossible to comprehend. He'd repeatedly told her he was doing these things so she could test her limitations and learn something about herself, and she had to admit that, in some hideously twisted fashion, he truly believed this to be the case. And what made it worse was that she lived in a society which regarded his behaviour as normal and hers as deviant. She could be sent to prison for making love to Yuke, but the state went out of its way to accommodate scum like Tyner, who had created elaborate philosophical rationales to justify torturing women. The British government had even perpetrated an act of mass murder to provide an excuse for the Hunt. As the pain between her legs increased, she began screaming at the top of her voice, "It's a nightmare! A nightmare! A nightmare! A nightmare! A nightmare!"

But there was nobody to hear her.

As the doctor predicted, she eventually started to feel numb, and by the time Tyner returned she barely cared whether or not she was released. Tyner looked up at her in admiration, saying, "I want you to know how proud I am. I'm going to take you down now." After undoing the leg restraints, Tyner grabbed hold of the rope and pulled Mara into the air. As she was abruptly wrenched away from the seat she'd occupied for the last eight hours, she cried out in agony. Tyner lowered her to the ground and untied her. She lay there in a foetal position, her hands pushed between her legs in a futile attempt to ease the pain. Tyner again stroked her hair and said, "Rest here for a while. I'll prepare some food." He was gone almost half an hour, but when he returned Mara still hadn't moved. He lifted her up, helped her into the robe, and gently led her out of the playroom.

Once again a pizza and a bottle of wine were sitting on the living room table. Mara sat down, groaning at the pain as she did so, and Tyner poured her a glass of wine. Filling his own glass, he raised it and said, "I propose a toast. To you, and your remarkable feat of endurance."

Mara wondered what would happen if she tried smashing the glass and twisting the jagged end in Tyner's face. She might cause quite a bit of damage before he managed to activate her collar. But she simply drank without acknowledging his presence.

"You're becoming a different person now, Mara," said Tyner as he gazed at her downturned face. "A much stronger person. I think you're starting to understand that."

Mara stared into her empty glass and said, "No. I'm not becoming a different person. You're destroying me. Soon there won't be anything left."

Tyner poured more wine into the glass in her hand. "We're going to build a new you in the ruins of the old."

Mara looked up at him and said, in a calm voice, "I preferred the old me. It was capable of loving and being loved. The old me was human. The new one sounds as if it's going to be a lifeless machine, like you. No emotions. No feelings. Have you ever had a relationship that didn't involve paying someone to let you beat them? The only emotion you're capable of is the desire for revenge. Women have ignored you all your life, and now you're making me pay for it."

Tyner's mouth twitched. Just a slight response, but there was no mistaking it. "Have some pizza," he said, almost pleadingly.

Mara shook her head. "I feel too sick to eat. You make me sick. May I go to bed now?"

Tyner stared grimly ahead, then stood up and brushed past Mara. Limping into the corridor, she found him standing by her bedroom, holding the door open. As she walked past him, he said, "I'm sorry you haven't yet grasped what I'm, like, trying to do. Perhaps what I have planned for tomorrow will make you understand." He shut the door softly.

Mara removed her robe, letting it drop to the floor, and went straight to the bathroom. She needed a shower. After drying herself, she lay on the bed curled in a ball, one hand protectively shielding her genitals, and drifted into a deep sleep in which she once again dreamed of a voice telling her to wake up. The voice sounded more familiar than ever, but she still couldn't identify it.

CHAPTER 13

Thursday March 29th

When Tyner came into the room on Thursday morning, Mara was already awake and wearing her robe. Before he had a chance to speak, she said, "Let's get this over with," and walked past him into the living room.

While Tyner busied himself in the kitchen, Mara sat on the sofa, trying to prepare herself for the day's ordeal. She noticed Tyner's mobile phone on the table, and thought of all those films she'd seen which showed women in peril desperately attempting to find a telephone so that they could summon help. Such logic clearly had no place here. Tyner didn't need to conceal his phone, since there was no possible use Mara could make of it. The idea of calling the police to report that she was being held prisoner by a sadist was obviously absurd. The police were there to protect the kidnapper, not the victim.

Without saying a word, Tyner placed the breakfast tray in front of Mara, then stood over her as she drank coffee and ate a slice of toast. "I know you're angry at me," he finally offered, "but that's because I'm breaking down the defences you've lived behind your entire life. It was inevitable you'd resent me for doing this."

Mara continued eating in silence. Taking a last swallow of coffee, she put down the cup and asked, "Are you ready?"

"Yes, ma'am," replied Tyner with a smirk.

As Tyner entered the playroom, Mara followed him in, removing her robe without waiting to be told and letting it drop to the floor. She was determined not to give Tyner the satisfaction of seeing her fear, which he seemed to drink as if it were a fine wine. Tyner walked towards a metal box about the size of a large suitcase, protected by a heavy padlock. Removing the padlock, he threw back the lid. Mara expected to see some dreadful torture device inside, but the box was empty. "Get in," commanded Tyner, and Mara understood how she was going to spend the rest of the day. She wanted to scream, to beg for mercy, but doing so would have no effect. Trying to appear as casual as possible, she stepped into the box and stood there staring into space. "Kneel down," said Tyner, and she did as she'd been ordered. By manipulating Mara until her head was between her knees and her hands clasped behind her neck, Tyner managed to fit her into the small space. Pushing her head down further, he said, "You'll be in here for eight hours," and closed the lid. Mara heard the sound of the padlock being returned to its original position. Pinpricks of light penetrated the airholes distributed evenly around the box's sides, but disappeared as Tyner pressed a button and plunged the playroom into darkness.

Mara heard a door slam, and knew she was now alone. After a few minutes, her whole body felt stiff, and she had trouble breathing. For the first time, she began to suspect she might not survive the Hunt. Tears poured down her face at the thought of never seeing Yuke again. But panicking used up more air, so she attempted to clear her mind. Perhaps, if she concentrated, she could separate herself from the pain rapidly spreading through every limb. She tried thinking of ideas for her next Melissa Valance novel, but the reality of physical discomfort soon pushed aside all merely cerebral concerns. Only the memory of Yuke's face, of the way she made love, of the way she felt, brought any solace, and as one minute stretched endlessly into the next, Mara started to imagine Yuke was actually there, wiping the sweat off her forehead and kissing her aching back. Sharing her pain. She could almost feel Yuke's weight. Over the next few hours, Mara passed in and out of consciousness, only intermittently aware of where she was. Is this what it's like to die? she wondered. By the time the padlock had been removed and the lid opened, she'd lost all contact with reality, and didn't notice she was no longer in the box until her limbs were suddenly permitted room to stretch, and pain once again surged through them. Mara realised she was being carried by two men, one of whom supported her upper arms while the other held her feet. She felt herself being dropped onto a bed, and heard a voice say, "Let me know when you've finished examining her." Then she was turned over on her stomach, and rough hands massaged her legs, her back, her arms. Mara became aware of Dr. Roberts standing over her, trying to restore circulation. She felt grateful, much as she despised the man. She closed her eyes, and when she opened them again she was alone in the dark room. She tried standing up, but immediately collapsed. Grasping the door handle, she pulled herself upright, and this time managed to remain on her feet. She limped slowly around the room, silently congratulating herself for having survived yet another performance in this theatre of torture. A hot shower helped clear her head, and as she dried herself, she heard a doorbell ring somewhere in the apartment, followed by the sound of voices. Hobbling out of the bathroom, she found her robe hanging by the door. She put it on and laid down. A sixth sense told her that something very bad was about to happen, something worse than anything she'd endured so far.

Approximately twenty minutes later, Tyner walked in, a serious look on his face. "Come with me," he said, in the tone of an executioner escorting a prisoner to the guillotine. "I have a surprise for you." Mara didn't want anything to do with Tyner's surprise, but she followed him anyway, knowing she had no choice.

Tyner led her to the playroom, opened the door, and stood aside to let her enter. What she saw so filled her with both relief and horror. Relief, because there, in the middle of the playroom, was Julie. Horror, because Julie was naked except for a collar, and standing in an impossibly rigid pose. Mara had taken considerable punishment over the last few days, and grown used to staring at her own beaten body in a mirror. But what she observed now rendered her speechless. Every inch of Julie's torso was covered in cuts, bruises and welts: dried blood was visible on her breasts and legs, and her stomach had been so savagely whipped that flaps of flesh hung loose from it. But more awful than any of this was the expression of naked terror on Julie's face. And standing just a few feet away was the source of that terror, Mr. Let's-Make-a-Deal, staring at Mara with a mixture of contempt and amusement. "Hello, Mara," he said coldly. "I'm so glad to see you again. I'm sure your friend is too."

Without removing his eyes from Mara, Let's-Make-a-Deal snapped his fingers. The instant he did so, Julie came to life, shaking off her rigid pose as if escaping from a spell cast by a wicked magician. She stumbled towards Mara, arms outstretched, crying, "Oh god, Mara, please help me. You don't know what...You have no idea...I..."

Mara put her arms around Julie and tried to calm her, saying, "Shhh. I'm here now. Everything's okay." But they both knew everything was far from okay.

Tyner had shut the door behind him, and was standing next to it with his hands in his pockets, silently watching. After allowing the two women to embrace for almost a minute, Let's-Make-a-Deal snapped his fingers twice, and Julie immediately stood erect again, swivelling around to face him. "Julie," he said, pointing towards the gynaecological examination chair, "sit there." Moving in an almost military fashion, Julie marched towards the chair, climbed onto it, and arranged her legs in the stirrups. Let's-Make-a-Deal began securing the leg restraints, while Tyner fastened the remaining straps. Mara could do nothing but look on helplessly. Once they'd finished, Tyner opened a white box Mara was familiar with and removed a handful of medical needles. To Mara's surprise, he held one of them out to her. Let's-Make-a-Deal glared at her, and said, "Unwrap that needle." Mara had some idea of what was about to happen, but did as she'd been ordered. Let's-Make-a-Deal smiled with satisfaction. "Good. Now I want you to use the object you have in your hand to pierce your friend's clitoris."

Mara felt the urge to vomit, but somehow controlled herself. "No," she said weakly. "You can't make me do that. I won't do it."

Let's-Make-a-Deal had obviously expected this response. "If you don't do what I've told you, I'll take three needles and stick all of them into this pathetic slut's clit." Mara could see there was no way out, and knew it would be more merciful to get this over with as quickly as possible. Trying to not think about what she was doing, she approached Julie, whose face was wide-eyed with dread, reached between her legs, squeezed her clitoris, and pushed the needle into it. Julie's cry of pain merged with Mara's cry of anguish.

Turning to Let's-Make-a-Deal, Mara asked, "May I take the needle out now?"

The man regarded her curiously, then said, "What would you do with it if you took it out? Throw it down the drain, like you did our trackers? Do you have any idea how lucky you were not to be caught by me? Still, Julie made an admirable substitute. I'm not permitted to lay a hand on you, but your friend here is another matter. The Hunt ends in sixteen hours, but I intend to make sure this vile cunt remembers tonight for the rest of her life."

Without waiting for a response, the man walked over to Julie, pulled the needle out of her clitoris, and threw it in Mara's face. With Tyner's assistance, he released Julie from the chair, and ordered her to get up. When she was once more standing rigidly erect, Let's-Make-a-Deal walked towards the door, gesturing for Julie to follow. Julie began to follow him, but suddenly, as if asserting one last remnant of free will, she ran towards Mara and kissed her on the cheek. With a roar of anger, Let's-Make-a-Deal tore across the room, grabbed Julie's wrist, and pulled her after him. As Julie was dragged away, she looked back and shouted, "Mara, I'm in the house now." The sound of the door slamming shut had a terrifying finality.

Tyner crept up behind Mara, and put his hand on her shoulder, saying, "You coped well with this test. And I think you just learned something that..."

Mara turned around and stared at Tyner. And what he saw in her eyes caused him to stop mid-sentence. Mara had been changed alright, but not in the way he'd expected. For the look she now directed at him was one of the purest hate imaginable. Mara thought she'd hated this man before, but what she felt now was something brand new to her: a hatred that could not possibly be put into words or given coherent expression, a hatred so all-encompassing it verged on madness. And the second he looked into her eyes, Tyner saw this hatred clear as day, saw it for what it was, understood that everything he'd ever been, everything he'd ever done, everything he ever would do, existed in the shadow of this hate, which had condemned him to a hell of loathing and contempt for as long as he lived. He tried to speak, but no words came. Mara understood exactly what Tyner had observed. She left the playroom, walked back to her bedroom, and waited for Tyner to let her in.

Mara did not sleep that night. She'd spent the last few days trying to shut out the reality of her situation, but now she let images of the horrendous spectacle in which she'd just participated flood her mind. She welcomed them, and encouraged them to stay. Her hatred spread until it covered her like a blanket. She knew that it would keep her warm, that it would be something she could rely on when the world chilled her to the bone.

She was still awake at dawn when Tyner entered the room and raped her. Neither of them said a word while it was happening, and as soon as he finished, the Hunter quietly departed, shutting the door behind him. After he'd gone, Mara took another shower.

CHAPTER 14

Friday March 30th

Mara lay awake through the early hours of the morning, feeding her hatred by thinking about what was being done to Julie. It must have been around ten a.m. when Tyner returned, carrying a tray which he left on the floor by the bed. He walked out without even glancing in Mara's direction. Mara looked down and saw that the tray contained a mug of coffee and four pieces of toast. For the first time since her arrival at the Hunters' block, she felt hungry. Her anger required plenty of sustenance. She drank the coffee quickly, though the heat burned her mouth, then consumed the toast, one piece after another.

Mara had expected Tyner to treat her to one last session in the playroom, but as the hours passed, she thought back on his recent behaviour, and concluded he was as eager as her to see the end of the Hunt. In some obscure way, she'd emerged as victor in this struggle. But the nature of the prize eluded her. Eventually, the door opened again, and Tyner came in, carrying a pile of clothes which he dropped onto the bed. He addressed Mara without looking directly at her.

"The Hunt will be over in an hour. You'd better put these on."

He didn't wait for a response, and probably knew Mara had no intention of making one. Once he'd left, Mara got out of bed and looked at the clothes. Her entire uniform was there. Every item, including the jacket, had been washed, though not ironed. Even the shoes were clean. She was soon sitting on the bed fully dressed.

Mara didn't have to wait long before the alarm was heard. The noise seemed to be coming from all around her. It lasted ten seconds. Tyner appeared almost immediately. He held the door open, and Mara walked out. As she passed him, the alarm sounded a second time, and Tyner placed a restraining hand on her shoulder. Mara shuddered as she wondered what he had planned, but he simply took a key out of his pocket and used it to unlock her collar. She saw a suitcase sitting by the apartment's front door, and couldn't help noting that it was almost the same size as the box in which she'd been locked. Tyner opened the front door and allowed Mara to pass through it. She walked over to the elevator and waited for Tyner to press the button. They were soon standing side by side as the elevator descended, Tyner's suitcase on the floor between them. Tyner turned to Mara and mumbled, "Thank you for a memorable few days. I hope I didn't hurt you more than was necessary, but I want you to know..."

"Shut up," hissed Mara.

Once they were outside, Mara strode swiftly down the street, Tyner trailing behind her. The alarm could be heard even more clearly out here. The sun was shining, and Mara tried to take pleasure in its warmth. But she was incapable of taking pleasure from anything. Looking back, she could see other pairings of Hunter and prey emerging from the building. When she arrived at the street's end, Tyner told her to go left. The alarm sounded one last time, then fell silent. Mara soon came to a part of the arena she recognised, and began moving more swiftly, hoping to put some distance between herself and Tyner. Turning into Kilburn High Road, she was surprised to see an unaccompanied woman strolling along ahead of her. Her spiky black hair looked familiar, and Mara ran to catch up. The woman proved to be Kate Mackendrick, the Scottish draftee who had travelled from Glasgow to participate in the Hunt. Kate hugged Mara, and asked how she was.

"I've been through hell," replied Mara honestly. "How about you?"

"I've just been bored. I found this old arts centre, and hid in an underground cinema there. I suppose it was out of range of the body heat detectors."

"How did you get food?"

"There was a vending machine outside. I felt terrified every time I used it, but nobody came by. You're the first person I've seen since last Friday. I was with a woman called Diane, but we lost each other while we were searching these empty houses, and I've no idea what happened to her."

Mara looked back at Tyner, who was standing further down the road, staring at her. She put an arm around Kate's shoulders, and the two of them marched towards the gate through which they'd entered the arena a week earlier. To their relief, it was open. Kate and Mara passed through the empty room where they'd been given their final instructions, and down the adjacent corridor. Tyner followed at a distance: he had the air of a naughty schoolboy on his way to the headmaster's office. Marching through the meeting hall - for Mara, at least, it stirred some extremely unpleasant memories - they made their way to the reception room.

The two police officers who had accompanied Isabella were waiting by the main entrance. To Mara, it seemed as if they'd been standing in the same position all week. And there was Simon - the lip-licking slob who'd tagged her - slumped against the receptionist's desk and evidently in a foul mood. Mara and Kate looked at each other, and immediately grasped the situation. Kate winked at Mara, walked over to Simon, and held out her hand. The man shook it instinctively, and Kate smiled at him as she said, "Hi, I'm the girl you've spent the last few days trying to find. Sorry we didn't get to know each other. But I hope you had a good time jacking off." She turned away with a big grin on her face. Simon just stood there, as if trying to process the information he'd received.

Mara couldn't resist rubbing it in. She went up to him and said, "Sorry I removed the tag you put on me. I dropped it into the sewer because I thought you'd feel more at home there." She walked back to Kate without waiting for a response, though Simon clearly didn't have the wit to formulate one. As Mara and Kate laughed, Tyner approached Simon and began talking sympathetically to him. Using a pen and paper borrowed from the receptionist, the two women exchanged email addresses, and after collecting her personal effects, Kate exited the stadium, giving Mara a friendly wave.

It wasn't long before the other Hunters showed up with their victims. The contrast between Kate and these tortured women was blatantly obvious. There were no mirrors in the reception area, but Mara could see the brutalisation that must be evident in her own eyes reflected in those of her fellow draftees. She recognised Zong, who shrunk away from her escort as if fearing another blow, and Isabella, who seemed to be in a state of shock; as soon as she appeared, the police officers handcuffed her and led her out of the building.

But where was Julie?

After being given the plastic bags containing their belongings, most of the women walked out without a backward glance. A certain amount of camaraderie existed between them at the start, but they obviously had no wish to spend a second more than necessary amongst people associated with the horrors they'd experienced. Curiously, the Hunters appeared to have left in much the same way. Mara hadn't even seen Tyner depart. As she approached the receptionist's counter, she noticed two men having an intense conversation in a room behind it. One of them seemed to be the escort who had welcomed them to the Hunt, but the other was concealed behind the doorway. As Mara tried to make out what they were saying, the second man moved into view. It was Let's-Make-a-Deal. And the bastard looked almost sheepish.

"Hey!" shouted Mara as loudly as possible, banging her fist on the counter. The two men stared at her. "Where's Julie?" she screamed. "Where is she?" The escort frowned and closed the door. Mara turned to the receptionist.

"Do you know what happened to Julie Weisz?"

The woman looked down at the counter, shaking her head. "I don't know. I...Can I get your things?"

Mara was far from satisfied, but she said, "My name's Mara Gorki." The receptionist fetched the bag containing Mara's belongings. As she handed them to her, Mara grasped the woman's hand and said, "Please. Julie's a friend of mine. I have to know if she's alright."

The receptionist glanced around nervously, checking to see if anyone was observing them, then leaned towards Mara and whispered, "I'm not supposed to discuss this yet, but everybody will know about it soon enough. One of the girls has died." She looked towards the cubbyholes and said, "Julie Weisz is the only one who hasn't collected her things, so it must be her. I...I'm sorry." Mara felt faint. She held onto the edge of the counter, using it to support her weight. As soon as she could move without collapsing, she shuffled towards the entrance.

Mara thought she'd had her fill of horror, but as she emerged from the stadium, she saw something that made her long for the oblivion of non-existence. For there, parked in front of the building, was a car containing a middle-aged couple who were looking around anxiously. Mara recognised them. They were Julie's parents, and they'd come to collect their beloved daughter. Mara understood what she had to do now, and realised it would take more courage than she'd ever known. As she approached the car, she remembered Catherine commenting on her bravery. She wasn't brave. Not at all. She desperately wanted to let those responsible for Julie's death break the news themselves. She could easily walk away. Nobody would even know. But that would be an act of cowardice for which she'd never forgive herself. Hand trembling, she knocked on the driver's side of the car. Julie's father lowered the window and smiled at her. "Yes?" he asked.

Mara had no idea what she was going to say. She opened her mouth, and her voice was choked with tears. "Oh, I'm so sorry. I'm so sorry. Julie...Julie didn't make it. I'm so sorry. She's dead...dead."

She tried to touch the man, whose expression had changed to one of anger and fear. "We'll see about that!" he barked, brushing away her hand and opening the car door.

As he strode towards the stadium, Mara glanced at the mother, and was met with a look of sheer hatred. "Why are you saying this?" shouted the woman, tears rolling down her face. "Why would you lie to us like this. Why? What kind of person are you?"

Mara's voice had almost gone. She could only whisper, "I'm sorry."

"Sorry? Sorry? You...you try to...you tell us a disgusting story about...about our daughter being dead and say you're sorry! Why do you hate us? Why do you want us to think...to think that...?"

She climbed out of the car and stood there shrieking at Mara. "You evil woman. Evil! Evil! Get away from me! Tell your filthy, disgusting lies to somebody else! Get away!" She crumpled into a ball, her face buried in her hands as she sobbed, "Please, get away from me. Oh, please!"

Mara wanted to comfort her, but at that moment the father ran out of the stadium, knelt down, and embraced his wife. "Please," he said, looking up at Mara. "Leave us alone. I beg you." He seemed almost calm. Without saying another word, Mara fled down the street, barely aware where she was going.

Once she'd put enough distance between herself and the bereaved couple, Mara slumped against a wall and screamed. She sat in this position for almost five minutes, sobbing uncontrollably. Several pedestrians stared at her, but nobody stopped to offer help. When she again felt capable of movement, she stood up and walked towards Hunt station, opening the plastic bag in her hand as she did so. She removed her mobile phone and the railcard, using the latter to pass through the turnstile. A train was pulling in when she arrived on the platform. As its doors closed behind her, she took a seat and switched on the mobile. There were several messages, but she couldn't deal with them now. Her first priority had to be letting Yuke know she was okay. No, she thought. Not okay. But alive. This part of the tube was still above ground, so she'd have no trouble making a connection. She entered her lover's number, and Yuke answered halfway through the first ring. "Mara," she gasped. "Is that you?"

Mara tried to steady her voice. "I've survived," she said simply. "I'm on my way home. I need you."

"I'll head out now. I'll be at your place in an hour."

"Make it two hours. And Yuke. It's better I say this now. It was bad. Maybe some day I'll tell you about it, but for now, please don't ask me."

"I love you," was the only thing Yuke said, and the only thing Mara needed to know. After ending the call, she sat back and tried to let the sound of the train moving away from the stadium soothe her. But as she closed her eyes, all she could hear was Julie singing.

"There is a house on the edge of town.
It's been there forever, so they say.
I've never once been inside it,
Though I pass it every single day.

My friends all believe it's haunted
By ghosts and spirits of the past.
But the only ghosts I'm afraid of

Are those of a life that will not last.

I know some day I must enter this house,
And leave behind everything that's me.
But until then I think I'll keep passing by,
Trying to pretend that I am free."

The Hunt was over.

BOOK 3
MARA GORKI
(AFTER THE HUNT)

CHAPTER 15

When she arrived home, the first thing Mara noticed was that her apartment had changed. Somebody appeared to have subtly rearranged everything. Yet, as far as she could see, all her belongings were exactly where she'd left them. She walked from room to room, trying to work out what had happened. Eventually, she realised the change was in her. The apartment felt strange because the last time she'd seen it, she had been a different person. In that sense, Tyner was correct. He had changed her. He'd introduced her to a chaos world in which she had no control over her body or what was done to it. But in the end she'd managed, in a way she still could not completely understand, to defeat him. And now she was determined to regain control of her life, to keep doing the things she'd done before, things that made her happy and fulfilled. Perhaps, if she went through the motions long enough, she would fall into a familiar rhythm, and eventually forget what she'd endured.

She could not face turning on her computer. She knew her inbox would be full of messages from friends desperate for news. They deserved an answer. But there would be time for that later. She removed her jacket and, as if in trance, hung it on a hook by the front door, kicking off her shoes as she did do. Then she unzipped her skirt and let it drop to the floor. She started undoing her blouse, but became frustrated and decided to rip it open, sending buttons flying in every direction. She threw the garment aside, and pulled off her tights, then her pants. She was now standing naked in the hall. Noticing the mail that had accumulated under her letterbox, she bent down and opened some of the envelopes and packages. Their contents seemed strange to her. Who had subscribed to this magazine, ordered this book, used the electricity this bill informed her she must pay for? Where had that woman gone? She went into the bathroom and examined herself in a full length mirror. The marks on her legs and stomach were already beginning to fade, but her back was still covered in welts, and the bruises on her buttocks showed no sign of clearing up. She felt a dull throbbing pain all over. She found a bottle of Amica cream in the cabinet over the sink. It helped a little, but also made the bruises look worse. Knowing she'd need to be examined by a doctor, she went into her office, called the Soho Medical Centre, and booked an appointment. Her brief conversation with the receptionist struck her as amusing in its banality, and she only just managed to stop herself giggling as the woman said, "We'll see you on Monday," in a cheerful voice which surely belonged to a world that had no connection with or knowledge of the one inhabited by Tyner. She wondered if the receptionist knew she'd been speaking to a naked woman. That struck her as even more amusing, and she let out a laugh which turned into a scream.

She ran a bath, hot as she could stand it. Leaving the bathroom door open so she could hear Yuke arrive, she immersed herself in the water and laid there for half an hour, sobbing quietly. When the doorbell rang, she climbed out and put on a robe which, for a moment, made her think of the one she'd worn in the Hunters' apartment. Dismissing this image with a shake of her head, she walked down the hall and opened the front door. Yuke was standing there, a concerned look on her face and a pizza box in her hand. She embraced Mara, set the pizza down on the living room table, and led her into the bedroom. A memory of Tyner leading her into the playroom clawed at the edges of her consciousness, but Mara refused to indulge it. Yuke didn't say a word as she pulled Mara onto the bed. She knew there was no point asking Mara how she was: the answer to that question became obvious as Yuke removed Mara's robe and saw the marks that covered her. After taking off her uniform, Yuke climbed into bed and began gently caressing Mara, avoiding the more obviously inflamed areas of her body. They made love for an hour, then lay side by side in a state of exhaustion, covered with sweat. The combination of the hot bath and the passionate sex had finally made Mara feel clean, as if the experiences of the past week were being washed away. Yuke sat up and kissed Mara on the lips., whispering, "I'll always be here for you. Just like this." It was the first thing she'd said since entering the apartment.

After five minutes of comfortable silence, Mara smiled weakly and asked, "Am I imagining things or did I see a pizza arrive with you?"

Yuke took a pair of jeans and a shirt from the wardrobe while Mara put her robe back on and went into the kitchen to warm the takeaway meal. The sight of pizza turning in the microwave, the machine's hum, the yellow glow it cast over the otherwise dark kitchen, the smell of food being heated, all these things struck Mara as reassuring signs of a return to safety. The Hunt was behind her, while a lengthy process of physical and psychological healing lay ahead. But for now, she felt curiously weightless, as if she had no obligations or concerns beyond eating with her lover. Whatever had happened before was irrelevant, whatever would happen after meaningless. She existed purely in the moment.

The two women were soon sitting on the living room sofa, leaning against each other and sharing junk food. Mara recalled eating pizza while sitting next to Tyner, but managed to push away the memory with surprising ease. That was the past. She watched Yuke nibbling at a crust, and felt a wave of admiration and love for her. The wounds she could not have helped seeing would have given Yuke a general idea of what had occurred, but she'd maintained precisely the combination of affectionate silence and normality Mara needed right now. The fact that Yuke's arrival with the usual Friday night pizza was intended to be perceived as a gesture - an indication that although things were far from normal at the moment, they soon would be - made it all the more touching and effective. But at some point, Yuke would need to know about the Hunt. Even the reality of Mara's ordeal could not be worse than the vague notions - terrifying because they had no clearly defined boundaries - that must currently be filling Yuke's head. And Mara needed to talk about certain things, Julie in particular.

Caressing Yuke's face, Mara said, "I'm going to tell you everything."

Yuke looked down, anxious not to meet Mara's gaze, and whispered, "I already know some of it. You were caught on Monday evening. He did something to your nipples. I could feel it. Not so strongly at that distance, but..." Both of them knew that their connection was not to be discussed directly, and when Yuke looked into her eyes again, Mara simply nodded. Yuke gripped her hand and said, "Tell me."

For the next two hours, Mara went through all the significant events of the past week. She tried to describe her torture in the most matter-of-fact way possible, leaving out nothing but not dwelling on details. By the time she finished, night had fallen. Yuke stroked Mara's hair and said, "It's over now. You're here with me. I'm going to heal you."

Just briefly, Mara felt Tyner stroking her hair as he asked, "Are you ready?"

They spent the rest of the evening in bed. Mara buried her face in Yuke's hair and cried for an hour. It seemed as if she might never stop, but eventually the tears ran out, and she felt purged. She made love to Yuke well into the early hours of the morning, and they fell asleep in each other's arms, just as they had the night their relationship began.

CHAPTER 16

Mara slept until almost noon on Saturday. When she awoke, she thought for a moment she was back in Tyner's apartment, in that terrifying bedroom where she'd awaited her tormentor. Yuke's presence swiftly returned her to reality. Her sleep had been completely dreamless, and she felt refreshed. She suspected Yuke had caught her nightmares. Yet Yuke now appeared to be resting peacefully. Yuke's left arm was wrapped around Mara, her hand on Mara's right breast. Mara caressed the stump where Yuke's little finger had once been. She hardly needed reminding of the brutality women's bodies were routinely subjected to by the state, but Yuke's disfigurement made her think of the pain they'd shared, and what that sharing implied. Yuke had certainly sensed, and to a degree felt, Mara's agony during the Hunt. She'd known exactly when the torture began, and which part of Mara's body was being abused. Their bond remained inexplicable, but to Mara it now seemed more real than ever, as real as the floors upon which she walked, never fearing they might prove illusory or incapable of sustaining her weight. She gently lifted Yuke's arm, being careful not to wake her, and slid out of the bed. Her uniform was lying on the floor in the hall, where she'd deposited it yesterday. She picked up the various items, and was about to place them in the washing basket when she changed her mind and decided to throw away everything except the shoes. She had a spare uniform, and wanted to get rid of anything associated with the Hunt. Tossing the skirt into the dustbin gave her a sense of satisfaction. She took a fresh pair of jeans and a jumper from the wardrobe: this was the first time she'd worn her own clothes in more than a week, and the cool denim felt good against her legs. Indeed, all her senses seemed strangely heightened, and as she walked down the hall towards the kitchen, she was aware of how comforting the soft carpet felt on her bare feet.

After making two large mugs of fresh coffee - not the instant she usually had for breakfast - and six slices of toast, she placed everything on a tray and carried it into the bedroom. Yuke was still sleeping. Mara took a piece of toast and held it under Yuke's nose. After a few seconds, Yuke laughed and opened her mouth wide. Mara allowed her to take a bite, then ate the rest of the slice herself. Yuke sat up, said, "Good morning," and began drinking the coffee, glancing nervously at Mara as she did so.

Mara looked her in the face and said, "I'm fine. Really." She was trying to put on a brave face for Yuke's benefit, but the truth was she did feel surprisingly good. She knew the full impact of what had happened would hit her full force in the near future, but at that moment her head was clear, the dull throbbing in the bruised areas of her body had magically vanished, and she felt ready to tentatively begin reengaging with the world. She decided to start by checking her email. She entered her office and turned on the computer. As Yuke looked over her shoulder, gently rubbing the back of her neck, Mara accessed her inbox and found sixty-three new messages. She deleted the obvious junk, and read some of the communiques from friends. They all struck much the same tone, urging her to contact them as soon as possible. Mara was touched by these expressions of concern. She composed a group email telling her friends she was recovering from the Hunt and hoped to see them all soon. This last remark was not merely a pleasantry: she really did want to see her friends soon, to bathe in the sanity they represented.

Mara spent an hour replying to the other emails, some of them business-related queries from her publisher, who had no idea what Mara was going through. Her editor loved *French Kill*, but required a few minor changes. And there was a message from Catherine Darden, who was back in New York, and wanted to let Mara know how much she'd enjoyed meeting her. She also noted that she'd enclosed the photos Mara had asked for. At first, Mara couldn't recall mentioning photos, but as she opened the attachment, her request came back to her. For there onscreen was a picture of a shelf with several Melissa Valance novels arranged in a neat row. A second attachment contained an image of the same shelf seen in a wider context, and a third showed a man standing behind the counter of a New York bookshop, holding a copy of *Kill Me Goodnight* in his left hand while making a thumbs up gesture with his right. Mara printed out the pictures, which Yuke pinned to the office wall, and wrote a reply thanking Catherine for her kindness.

Mara wondered if Julie's death had been reported by what laughably passed for Britain's 'news media'. She remembered the receptionist saying, 'Everybody will know about it soon enough.' She accessed the *Daily Male*'s website, and was not surprised to find a headline about rising house prices. Subsequent pages contained the usual mixture of celebrity gossip and anti-immigrant rabble-rousing; the fact that there were no longer any immigrants in the country had not stemmed the flow of these manufactured stories in the slightest. But on page eight was a piece entitled "Accidental Death of Hunt Participant."

"Julie Weisz, 21, died yesterday morning while participating in a Hunt. At the time of her death she was in the custody of Robert Price, 43, who is currently being questioned by the police. David Wainwright, Head of Hunt Administration, insists that Mr. Price is simply assisting the police with their enquiries, and that a preliminary investigation suggests there is no reason to suspect him of wrongdoing. According to Mr. Wainwright, 'We at the Hunt make every effort to ensure rules concerning safety are adhered to, and we are proud of our record. Thousands of women have taken part in the Hunt, and this is the first serious incident which has occurred.' A postmortem on Miss Weisz's body will be carried out later today."

Mara shook her head, and Yuke, who was reading over her shoulder, said, "The bastards!" A Google search revealed that coverage in other online 'newspapers' conveyed essentially the same information. Mara felt as if a wave of cold air had swept through the apartment. She switched off the computer and embraced Yuke, welcoming the warmth of her body. Mara was determined to perform the usual weekend rituals, though this was now very much a performance in the theatrical sense of the word. She spent the rest of the day watching DVDs and ordering food. She was ravenously hungry, and the more she ate, the hungrier she became. Her body was clearly making up for its lack of sustenance during the past week, and Mara, who knew hunger to be a sign of good health, indulged herself with excessive amounts of chicken and pizza. By the time evening arrived, she felt close to bursting, and Yuke, who had only sampled the odd slice here and there, was obviously delighted. They went to bed and held each other close. It occurred to Mara that she really had survived her ordeal, both mentally and physically, and was well on the way to recovery.

CHAPTER 17

Mara had what appeared to be a dreamless night, and again slept until noon. Yuke also seemed to have rested peacefully, but as she sat up in bed eating the breakfast prepared by Mara, she obviously had something on her mind. At Mara's coaxing, she confessed what it was.

"I can't stop thinking about that letter. The one suggesting the 2059 bombings were carried out by the government."

Mara nodded. "Of course," she admitted, "the letter doesn't prove anything, but..."

"But you know it's true."

Mara sighed. "But I know it's true."

"And that poor girl. Julie. She died because of this. Because the state killed more than a hundred people just to provide an excuse for torturing women. Mara, it can't be true! The world can't really be like this!"

Mara tried to think of something reassuring she could say, but nothing came. And constantly present in the back of her mind was the knowledge that Yuke could be conscripted into the Hunt at any moment.

They remained in bed for the next few hours, but even as they made love, Mara was overwhelmed by depression. She'd been in an almost euphoric state yesterday, but now felt herself swinging to the opposite end of the emotional spectrum. As always, Yuke was sensitive to her every mood. Sitting up in bed, she said, "I think I should stay over one more night."

Mara looked at her gratefully. "I wish you could stay over every night. But at some point I'll need to confront what I've been through by myself."

Yuke hesitated, as if nervous about what she planned to do, then leaned over and whispered, "I promised to heal you. You need another night of dreamless sleep. Let me catch your nightmares."

Mara gasped in surprise. This was the first time either of them had unambiguously referred to their mysterious bond, and it felt as if a bridge had been crossed. She embraced Yuke and said, "It's okay, you don't have to whisper. Whatever this thing is, it's very real and very solid. It won't be destroyed that easily."

An expression of relief spread across Yuke's face. She held up her left hand, with its missing digit, and said, "I know what you did for me."

"But I didn't always know what you were doing for me. You seemed to be sleeping peacefully the last two mornings. In the past, I've always been able to tell when you were dreaming for me."

"Your last few dreams must have taken place while you were in REM sleep. They were long over by the time you woke up."

Mara could hardly believe they were discussing their connection as if it were a practical tool, one which could be picked up and examined. But now that they'd taken the plunge, there was no turning back. "How did you know the dreams were mine? How could you be certain they weren't yours?"

"I always feel like I'm observing my dreams from afar, as if I was watching a film. Sometimes a terrifying film, but still a film. You always seem to be directly involved in your dreams. It's the strangest thing I've ever experienced. When I have your dreams, I feel like I'm you, but when I have my dreams, I don't feel like me. I'm not even sure that makes sense. I'm not sure any of this makes sense."

"I've heard of identical twins who knew what their siblings were experiencing, even if they were in different countries. What we have must be like that in some way. But it's real enough. You couldn't have simply guessed what happened to me last Monday. Will you...Will you tell me what I dreamed?"

"The dreams you had on Friday were very fragmentary. There was a girl singing, and a woman telling you to wake up. I couldn't see the woman, only hear her. Then you were sitting on a chair in a dark room. A man was standing over you. He told you he couldn't remember anything that happened in the past, and he had to destroy you, because you could remember. Then you told him he didn't exist. He became angry and threatened to take the thing you valued most. When you looked up, you saw there was a mirror where his face should have been. Then...then I appeared, and I started shouting at you, insisting I didn't know who you were. Does this mean anything to you?"

"I've been dreaming about a woman telling me to wake up for weeks now. And the singing girl must be Julie. She's not actually a girl, she's twenty-one...she was twenty-one. But I thought of her as a girl. The dark room must be the playroom, and the man might have been Tyner. Otherwise, I don't understand that part. The stuff about not remembering the past and the mirrored face mean nothing to me. You not knowing who I am...that sounds familiar, but I can't quite grasp it. Maybe it's a dream I've had before."

"I may not be remembering that part correctly. I'm thrown out of your dreams whenever I appear in them. And all these images were bundled together, so there wasn't a clear line between one dream and another, or one person and another. I think I was merging with the singing girl. The dream you had last night was much more coherent. You're standing naked in a small bedroom, waiting for somebody to appear. Eventually, the door opens, and a man walks in. Fat, balding, probably in his forties. He's wearing a T-shirt with the words Dukes of Death Metal printed on it."

"Tyner!" said Mara. "That's the T-shirt he had on the day he caught me. When I told you about the Hunt, I didn't describe it to you."

Yuke took a deep breath and continued. "He handcuffs your hands behind your back, and attaches a leash to the collar you have around your neck. He firmly grips the end of the leash and leads you out of the room, into a hallway, through a door, into a corridor, down in a lift, across a lobby, through another door. Then you're standing on a road lined with half-destroyed buildings. You see four or five other women - all naked, all with their hands cuffed behind their backs - walking ahead of you, each one following a man holding a leash. You're all heading towards a large gate. Once you pass through this gate, you're taken into a reception area. A woman sitting behind a counter shouts, 'Don't forget your belongings,' but the man, Tyner, just drags you through the main entrance and into a street. At first, it seems to be a normal London street. Turning towards Tyner, you ask, 'Why have we left the stadium?' and he says, 'We're still in the stadium.' Then you ask, 'Is the Hunt over?' and he replies, 'The Hunt will never be over.' You suddenly realise the street is full of bound and naked women, hundreds of them, being led on leashes by men. Tyner keeps walking until he comes to a restaurant. He ties you to a post outside, then goes in and sits at a table. You watch him through the window as he eats a large meal: a starter, main course, wine, dessert, coffee. When he finishes, he comes out and drops a piece of meat onto the filthy pavement in front of you. You get down on your knees and devour it hungrily. That's when the dream ends."

Mara began to cry. She threw her arms around Yuke and said, "It's an awful dream. Thank you for protecting me from it. But tonight, I need to start having my own dreams again."

It was almost time for Yuke to catch the train back to East Finchley. As she put on her uniform, she said, "If you need to talk in the night, call me."

Mara felt sadder than ever to see Yuke go. It was as if a part of her own body had been ripped away. Trying to take her mind off Yuke's absence, she decided to check her email again. There were messages from friends, who expressed their joy that she was safe. Some of them suggested getting together for a drink the following weekend. Mara dreaded the inevitable questions, but she longed for normal company, and decided she'd arrange something within the next few days. Bringing up the *Daily Male* website, she scrolled from page to page, searching for more information about Julie. And there, in a relatively prominent position, was a report headlined "Hunt Death Due to Natural Causes."

"Julie Weisz's death during a Hunt occurred due to natural causes, according to a pathologist's report. Dr. Frederick Letap, who conducted the postmortem examination, concluded that Miss Weisz died of a heart attack. 'Her heart was weak,' claimed Dr Letap, 'and she could have died any time. That she happened to pass away during a Hunt was simply a coincidence.' Dr. Alex Roberts, the physician who examined Miss Weisz on a daily basis while she was participating in the Hunt, insisted, 'Miss Price was coping admirably, and hadn't been treated any differently than the other contestants. It's not usual for twenty-one-year-olds to die of heart-related illnesses, but it does happen, and nobody connected with the Hunt is in any way to blame.' Robert Price, in charge of Miss Weisz at the time of her death, expressed his sympathies to her family. 'Julie was a great girl, and I enjoyed getting to know her. I knew I'd done nothing wrong, but it's a relief to have this confirmed officially.'"

Mara thought back to her encounter with Let's-Make-a-Deal - or Robert Price, as he seemed to be named - recalled his twisted face as he hissed, "I intend to make sure this vile cunt remembers tonight for the rest of her life." She recalled Julie being dragged away, screaming "I'm in the house now," knowing she was going to die. And she looked again at the *Daily Male* article, which claimed this healthy young woman had suffered a heart attack. The fact that Julie's heart attack occurred while she was being tortured must have been purely coincidental! Indeed, from the tone of the article, one might have assumed Julie and Price spent their time together drinking tea. Given what Mara now knew about 2059, none of this surprised her. But surely there was a way to reveal the truth: if not about the bombings - most people would refuse to accept that - then at least about what took place during a Hunt. Sensitive information was once spread via the Internet, but following a series of high-profile whistleblower incidents earlier in the century, the world wide web had been ring-fenced so that only information approved by the government could be viewed in the U.K..

The last time Mara had seen Julie's parents, they'd begged her to leave them alone. Was it her responsibility to tell them what really happened? Or would it be better to let them think their daughter died peacefully? They had a right to know the truth; but how could they possibly cope with it? She vividly remembered the day she'd discovered the corpses of her own parents, lying side by side in their bed. The memory filled her with sadness. But losing one's parents belonged to the natural order of things, even if suicide hardly counted as a natural death. Losing a daughter was something else entirely, a horror beyond contemplation. Mara felt an almost palpable connection to the Weiszs. One way or another, they were all victims of the Hunt. She took the Hunt pamphlet from the drawer where she'd deposited it, and read the section towards the end, which claimed, "Any Hunter whose behaviour results in the death of a captive will be prosecuted to the fullest extent of the law." Mara laughed sardonically. Price would not be seeing the inside of a courtroom any time soon.

Mara started going through the list of changes her editor required in the manuscript of *French Kill*. As usual, the suggestions were intelligent and respectful of Mara's intentions, aimed only at clarifying the narrative and eliminating inconsistencies. Mara was appalled to discover that, during the period in which she'd been working on the novel with the threat of the Hunt looming over her, she'd become so distracted she had revived a character killed off earlier, and provided two hopelessly contradictory backstories for the victim. She spent the rest of the evening making the necessary alterations, thankful she'd only embarrassed herself before her editor rather than her readers. She sent off the corrected draft around two in the morning, and collapsed into bed with the feeling of a job well done. As she closed her eyes, she mentally prepared herself for the nightmares which seemed inevitable now that Yuke was gone.

CHAPTER 18

When Mara awoke on Monday morning, she was pleasantly surprised to find that, so far as she could tell, she'd had another dreamless night's sleep. She wondered if Yuke were in some way responsible. A less pleasant surprise awaited her when she tried sitting up in bed, and discovered the dull throbbing pain she'd felt on Friday had returned. It was less severe than before, but still irritating. Yet she'd been fine over the weekend. Yuke had obviously shared her pain as well as her nightmares. Apparently, their gift worked both ways. Mara wondered if she'd ever caught Yuke's dreams without being aware of it.

Now that she was alone in the apartment, Mara tried returning to her usual morning routine, but all the commonplace actions - making breakfast, checking email, reading a few chapters of a book before starting the day's work - felt curiously abstract. It was as if she were taking part in a kabuki play. She'd attended a kabuki performance at the Barbican once with Yuke, who'd explained to her how kabuki theatre was created by a woman, Izumo no Okoni, and acted entirely by female performers: that is until the Tokugawa Shogunate passed a law banning women from participating. Since then, all kabuki roles, including female ones, had been enacted exclusively by males. There were so many similar examples of women being erased from history that what was happening in Britain today seemed almost inevitable.

Mara continued thinking about the kabuki as she changed into her uniform, which now reminded her of those elaborately artificial costumes she'd seen onstage. She was intensely conscious of the fact that these clothes represented not her natural self, but rather an externally imposed feminine role assigned her by the state. It was absurd to be concerned about such a seemingly trivial thing, especially given the enormity of what she'd recently endured, but she resented the uniform more than ever. To her, it was the oppression from which all the other oppressions emanated. She remembered how good she'd felt while putting on her jeans two days ago, and knew this feeling to be imbricated with the freedom of choice such an act implied. Now, as she buttoned the regulation blouse, pulled on the regulation tights, and stepped into the regulation skirt, her mood turned black. She perceived her body as something no longer her own. Every movement she made in the course of donning the uniform had been dictated by the representatives of an ideology she despised, and whom she obeyed solely because she feared punishment. Even the action of moving her hands behind her back so she could zip up the skirt struck her as somehow puppet-like, and summoned a memory of Tyner binding her arms in this position. She wished she could stay home, but she'd made an appointment at the Soho Medical Centre for two-thirty, and the nagging ache in those parts of her anatomy which had suffered abuse suggested it was high time she consulted a doctor.

Stepping out the front door, Mara experienced a sense of anxiety. She couldn't help recalling the last time she'd left the apartment, on her way to the Hunt. She didn't want her entire life to be defined by those seven days, but there was no denying she'd been changed. She'd always suspected the world of being a dangerous and terrifying place. Now she knew it to be so. She needed to steel herself just to make one foot move in front of the other and carry her down the road towards St. Pancras. The weather had turned cold again, and as she passed through the tube station's turnstile and descended the escalator, Mara stared enviously at the men in their warm trousers. Why, she wondered, did having penises give them the right to keep their legs covered? The penis must be a truly magical piece of flesh, since it also enabled its owners to vote, to drive, to leave the country. To not be tortured. It occurred to Mara that almost everyone in the station was male. A few women were scattered here and there, but certainly no more than five or six in an area currently containing at least a hundred people. The extent to which females had been discouraged from entering public spaces became more apparent with each passing day. Women comprised half the population, yet increasingly seemed like a minority group. Mara felt nervous as she took a seat on the train, although none of the men surrounding her looked threatening. They were mostly interacting with electronic devices or reading newspapers. Mara realised she didn't have anything to read. Why had she forgotten to bring a book? Did she subconsciously fear someone might rip it apart? She was learning society's lessons well. Perhaps she'd eventually become a model citizen. Her emotions were in a turmoil, lifting her to the heights of ecstasy, then dragging her to the depths of depression. She was overjoyed to have survived the Hunt. And she wished she were dead.

These dark thoughts were still on Mara's mind when she arrived in Soho, where the street priests subjected her to torrents of verbal abuse. She almost responded to the one who shouted, "Slow down, you cunt! You'll get to Hell quick enough!" but just managed to stop herself in time: insulting a priest could easily have cost her a finger.

Walking through the doors of the medical centre, Mara noticed Dr. Rodman standing in the reception area, saying goodbye to a patient. He waved at Mara and showed her into his consulting room. "You look like you're in one piece," he observed cheerfully as she sat down.

"If only you could see what's going on inside," thought Mara, but she smiled in a friendly fashion. She wasn't currently very impressed by members of Dr. Rodman's profession, but there was no reason to blame him for the activities of his colleagues.

The doctor suggested Mara remove her clothes and lay down on the examination couch. After examining the bruises on her breasts, stomach and legs, he said, "Turn over please, Miss Gorki." Mara was touched by the sympathy in his voice. She heard him tut-tutting as he observed the damage caused by Tyner. When the examination had been completed, the doctor made a few notes as Mara put her uniform back on. She noticed him pressing his pen down so heavily it made jagged gashes in the paper, and suspected this was something he habitually did to avoid thinking about potentially disturbing subjects. When Mara was fully dressed, Dr. Rodman asked how she felt.

"I'm still very sore, but the pain is easing a little."

"You should have come to see me as soon as the Hunt was over. I'll give you a prescription for some cream. I want you to apply it to the wounded areas twice a day for a week. I assume you've been using painkillers." Mara couldn't help laughing at this. Little did the doctor know she had access to a brand of painkiller which was much more effective than any of those available for sale. As he typed the relevant information into his computer, Dr. Rodman said, "I suggest you get in touch with the...the person who...did these things to you and make him take care of your medical costs. He's legally obliged to do so, and Hunt Administration will give you his contact details."

"Frankly, I'd rather not have anything more to do with him."

The doctor frowned. "It's possible there will be some scarring on your buttocks. If the scars are still evident six months from now, you may have grounds to sue." Mara thanked the doctor and left. Only when she was halfway down the road did she realise she'd forgotten to pay. It didn't matter, of course. She could easily settle the bill when she got home.

Since she had nothing to read on the return journey, Mara decided to visit Charing Cross Road and search for *The Stand*, the second book in a row somebody had prevented her from finishing. She hadn't managed to track down a replacement copy of *The Aging Boy* anywhere, even online, but didn't anticipate any difficulties locating this popular Stephen King novel. She spent half an hour browsing in Henry Pordes' basement section, with its reassuringly musty smell, and soon found not just a good-quality paperback of *The Stand*, but also a three-volume edition of Robert Musil's *The Man Without Qualities*, which she'd been wanting to read for years, and *The SCUM Manifesto* by Valerie Solanas. Leaving the shop, she happily clasped the plastic bag containing her purchases, pleased to discover that books still had the power to give her pleasure, that she was still the same person she'd been before the Hunt.

As she made her way into Leicester Square station, it struck Mara as important she not ride in an empty carriage. She knew it was illogical to think this way, but she desperately wanted to avoid another encounter with those gangs of young men who prowled the tube looking for helpless women to abuse, and a crowd seemed to offer more protection. In the end, the train turned out to be so full she couldn't even find a seat. Since she didn't like to read standing up, her books remained in their bag.

Upon returning to St. Pancras, Mara visited the local Superdrug and filled her prescription. The chemist handed her a large jar of something called Hunex: according to the packaging, it was "ideal for Hunt trauma." As soon as she arrived home, Mara took off her uniform and went into the bathroom. She hadn't examined her body since Friday, and was appalled by what she now saw. She looked as if she'd been in a car crash. She opened the jar of Hunex, and applied the white cream it contained to her buttocks and back, then to the other sore areas. The cream stung at first, but after a few seconds the throbbing pain she'd been experiencing all day vanished. Mara almost wept with relief. Physically, she now felt fine. But those wounds not visible on the surface would be much more difficult to treat. That aspect of 'Hunt trauma' would not be soothed by even the most miraculous cream.

After easing herself into jeans and a jumper, Mara entered her office, sat in front of the computer, and checked to see if there were any more pieces about Julie in the *Daily Male*. She soon discovered an item on page eight, ungrammatically headlined "Parents of Hunt Death Woman Refuses to Accept Verdict."

> "The parents of Julie Weisz, who died on Friday while taking part in a Hunt, have announced they will not accept the pathologist's verdict that their daughter's death occurred due to natural causes. The family's lawyer, Aaron Rosenbaum, has issued a statement demanding that a full investigation be launched into what happened during the final hours of Miss Weisz's life, and that another postmortem be carried out. Robert Price, in charge of Miss Weisz at the time of her death, expressed his shock at the news: 'My heart goes out to Julie's family, but I am an innocent man.'"

It was only a small piece, but the words 'See editorial on page 12' appeared at the bottom of the text. Mara located the editorial, which was almost four times as long as the article.

"The death of a young woman is always a tragedy. But people die every day in car crashes, in household accidents, and from good old natural causes. According to accredited forensic pathologist Dr. Frederick Letap, Julie Weisz's death was the result of heart failure. Case closed? Apparently not. Because Miss Weisz happened to pass away while participating in a Hunt. And the Weisz family, clearly recognising a golden opportunity, seems determined to milk this cow for all it's worth. Their lawyer, Aaron Rosenbaum, has demanded an investigation be launched (at the taxpayers' expense) and another postmortem carried out. We have every sympathy for the loss suffered by these parents, but somebody needs to tell them that autopsies and investigations will not bring their daughter back. We would never dream of suggesting that individuals with such venerable British names as Weisz and Rosenbaum might be salivating at the thought of financial compensation, but if the family has anything else to gain, we frankly have trouble seeing what it is.

Inevitably, the actions of the family Weisz and the firm Rosenbaum will have Marxist-Feminist busybodies clamouring for a ban on the Hunt. But the Hunt has served this country well. It was created to remind terrorists that their activities would not be tolerated, and would have a negative impact on the very communities they claimed to represent. The fact that not a single terrorist attack has been launched in the U.K. since the Hunt's introduction testifies to its success.

> Julie Weisz was a victim, yes, but a victim of a weak heart. The real victim here is Robert Price, the gentleman who had the bad luck to find himself in charge of Miss Weisz at the time of her death. Like Iago, the Weiszs will not be satisfied until they have collected their pound of flesh. But we fear Mr. Price will not be the last innocent victim in this case. For banning the Hunt might prove more expensive than anyone suspects. And the cost will be paid in blood."

Mara didn't know whether to be infuriated or overjoyed by this editorial. The undisguised antisemitism and the determination to portray a sadistic killer as a victim of injustice revolted her, but they were more or less par for the course. This was, after all, a publication which had supported Adolf Hitler and Oswald Mosley. And what could anyone reasonably expect from an editor who confused Iago with Shylock? But right there, on the editorial pages of a widely read newspaper, was the suggestion that the Hunt might be banned. The suggestion may have been made as part of a pro-Hunt argument, but the fact it had been made at all seemed significant and encouraging. The end of the Hunt. That was something worth fighting for.

There would be little point telling the police what she knew about Julie and Price. But perhaps this lawyer, Aaron Rosenbaum, could make use of the information. Mara wondered how she should approach him. She trusted her own lawyer, Madeleine Danes, implicitly, and decided to ask her advice. Calling Madeleine's office, she made an appointment for the following Monday.

Mara felt like relaxing and getting back to *The Stand*, but she decided to check her emails first. As she accessed her inbox, the message from Stephen Tyner caught her attention. Mara's hand shook as she opened it.

"From: Big Steve2019@yahoo.com
To: Mara.Gorki@aol.com
Subject: The Hunt hi Mara, i just wanted to let yu no that i really enjoyed the time we spent together. i no you did not like some of the things we did,but im sure once euve had a chants to think about it yu will admit i was rite and yu now no more about eureself than yu did bee four. i would like to see yu agen so we can play sum more. but dont wurry. weel have a safe word this time (unless yu dont want one). i no i said i would report yu for been out of uniform,but if yu were willing to play with me sum more i would forget about the hole thing.
Stephen Tyner p.s. i was sorry to here about ure frend dine. i only met her breefly but she seemed like a nice persun."

A picture was attached to the message. It showed Mara standing on a street in the Hunt arena, wearing jeans and a jumper, a collar visible around her neck. Mara was appalled, though more by Tyner's spelling than anything else. This lunatic genuinely believed she'd want to see him again, and even thought he could blackmail her into doing so! The man's stupidity was almost as astonishing as his sadism. She suddenly remembered she'd not paid her bill at the clinic: as Dr. Rodman had pointed out, Tyner was responsible for her medical expenses. She hadn't wanted to contact Hunt Administration and ask for Tyner's contact details, but since she had them in front of her, she might as well use them.

"To: Big Steve2019@yahoo.com
From: Mara.Gorki@aol.com
Subject: Re: The Hunt
If you ever try to contact me again, I will call the police.
You are legally required to pay all expenses

relating to injuries I suffered as a result of your activities. Call Soho Medical Centre immediately. There is already an unpaid bill you need to take care of. I will instruct the clinic to send future bills to you directly.

You're right. Julie was a nice 'persun'. It's too bad you and 'ure frend' destroyed her."

Feeling satisfied with her response, Mara hit 'send'. After turning off the computer, she went into the living room and settled down on the sofa with *The Stand*. She had no trouble locating the page she'd been on when her reading was interrupted. She feared the book would bring back memories of the circumstances under which she'd discovered it, but Stephen King's fictional world had its own power, and she was soon immersed in the narrative again. She read all day, stopping only to make herself a salad - junk food was strictly for weekends - and, after using some more Hunex, continued reading in bed. She fell asleep with the book in her hand, just fifty pages from the end. And for the first time in days, she dreamed. It was the recurring dream of a familiar voice begging her to wake up. But this voice was also saying something else now. "Once into the Hunt. Twice into the Hunt. Then all will be revealed. Once into the Hunt. Twice into the Hunt." Mara now perceived that the voice belonged to a woman, but the woman's identity remained tantalisingly out of reach.

CHAPTER 19

Mara finished reading *The Stand* the following day, and felt inspired to start work on her next Melissa Valance novel. She knew this was going to be a difficult one, involving as it did Melissa participating in the Hunt. Mara was having problems outlining the book, since she couldn't see how to combine the Hunt with a murder investigation. She was not blind to the irony. Here she was peripherally involved with a real-life murder investigation related to the Hunt, yet she had trouble finding a way to convey her experience via the generic fiction she specialised in. The problem from a dramatic viewpoint was more or less identical to the problem from a legal viewpoint: so far, the murder investigation was conspicuous by its absence. Perhaps she could write a semi-autobiographical book, inventing an ending in which Melissa exposes the truth and brings the bad guys to justice. Of course, the real bad guys were not the two sadists primarily responsible for Julie's death, but the entire system supporting and encouraging them. And that was certainly a theme worthy of Melissa Valance. Mara decided she'd at least attempt to write it that way, beginning with Melissa receiving a draft notice.

Mara wrote for hours, and by six-thirty had completed an opening chapter, though one which dissatisfied her. She couldn't put her finger on it, but something was missing. She knew full well that, much as she'd have loved to be Melissa Valance, she was nothing like her. Although the books were reticent on the subject of Melissa's heterosexuality - the private detective's nominal boyfriend, like Lieutenant Columbo's wife, was referred to occasionally, but never actually appeared - it was difficult to imagine her spending the weekend eating pizza and watching DVDs with her lesbian lover.

The idea of watching a DVD seemed more appealing than continuing with writing that lacked spontaneity. Mara had only recently turned in her last novel, and there was no pressing need to rush into a new one. If she was going to write about the Hunt, she wanted to do so with the experience fresh in her mind. But perhaps a little distance was needed before she could transform reality into fiction. She saved what she'd written so far, made a fish dinner, and settled down to watch Dorothy Arzner's *Dance, Girl, Dance*, a film she'd loved ever since seeing it on television as a child.

When the film was over, Mara applied some more Hunex to her bruised body, climbed into bed, and looked at the other books she'd purchased yesterday. *The Man Without Qualities* promised to demand more concentration than she felt capable of giving it at the moment, so she picked up *The SCUM Manifesto*, which, at less than fifty pages, was virtually a pamphlet. Mara had heard of this book, and knew about its author trying to kill Andy Warhol, but she was unprepared for the essay's satirical brilliance. It was written one-hundred years ago, yet Valerie Solanas had already perceived that no aspect of life was "at all relevant to women," and could see what the sexism of the world she inhabited would eventually lead to. The book's introduction explained that Solanas was not being serious when she proposed forming a Society for Cutting up Men, dedicated to destroying the male sex. But Mara assumed the writer was simply pursuing an idea to its logical conclusion. If Solanas' analysis of masculine oppression was correct, and subsequent events suggested it was, then women would need to be just as ruthless as their oppressors if they wished to survive. It was kill or be killed. Mara was especially impressed by Solanas' account of the typical male, "completely egocentric, trapped inside himself, incapable of empathizing or identifying with others, of love, of friendship, affection or tenderness. He is a completely isolated unit, incapable of rapport with anyone. His responses are entirely visceral, not cerebral; his intelligence is a mere tool in the service of his drives and needs; he is incapable of mental passion, mental interaction; he can't relate to anything other than his own physical sensations. He is a half dead, unresponsive lump, incapable of giving or receiving pleasure or happiness...trapped in a twilight zone halfway between humans and apes." Mara shuddered as she read this. It could have been a description of Tyner.

On Wednesday morning, Mara continued writing the book she was calling *A Kill is Just a Kill*. She'd decided to make Melissa's response to the Hunt letter more or less duplicate her own, introducing fictionalised characters based on Claire Richardson and Dr. Rodman. But the more she wrote, the more she became aware of the disparity between herself and Melissa. She was making her heroine behave in ways which didn't gel with the persona established in previous novels. And Mara couldn't forget that the real story had yet to be resolved. Every so often she'd check online to see if there were any further reports about Julie, but 'The Weisz Case' had been pushed aside to make way for more important 'news' items concerning rumours of a Hollywood star's divorce.

Around three o'clock, Mara became so frustrated that she decided to take a break and pay Yuke a surprise visit. She changed into her uniform, put the jumper and jeans she'd been wearing, as well as the jar of Hunex, into a backpack, and set out for the tube station. She hadn't been to East Finchley in almost a year, and felt excited by the prospect of seeing Yuke's small but warm living space again. She arrived at Yuke's apartment building just after four, and pressed the buzzer. Yuke answered right away, and gave a squeal of delight as Mara announced herself. When Mara stepped out of the elevator, Yuke was standing in her doorway looking happy but concerned.

"Is everything alright?" she asked. Mara shut the door behind her.

"Work wasn't going well, so I thought I'd recharge the batteries by coming to see you. I'm not disturbing you, am I?"

Yuke responded by pulling Mara into the bedroom and removing her clothes. "This is how much you're disturbing me," said Yuke as she buried her head between Mara's thighs. Mara never failed to be astonished by how sexually compatible they were. Her heterosexual friends seemed rather equivocal about the physical aspects of their relationships, and Mara had difficulty relating to their lack of passion.

As the two women laid back on the bed, breathing heavily, Mara surveyed the room, which looked much as it had the last time she'd been there. All four walls were covered with bookshelves, a complete set of Melissa Valance novels occupying a privileged position in the bedside cabinet. Yuke had asked Mara to sign each one, and though she felt awkward signing books for somebody so close to her - it was almost like signing them to herself - she'd happily complied, requesting an autographed copy of Yuke's *Devious Ways: American Cinema and the Twentieth Century* in return.

While Yuke used the phone beside her bed to call the local takeaway, Mara retrieved the backpack she'd dropped by the front door and went into the bathroom. She applied the Hunex, though she no longer seemed to need it, and put on the clothes she'd brought with. After using the toilet, she wandered into the living room, which was also lined with shelves, these containing Yuke's extensive collection of DVDs. The computer screen was still illuminated, and Mara saw that Yuke had been working on an article entitled "Mizoguchi's Cinema of Empathy."

As Yuke, now fully dressed, came in, Mara said, "Honey, I'm really sorry I interrupted you. If you like, I can leave after we've eaten."

Yuke looked at her seriously. "Last week was so awful. I felt what that man was doing to you every day. You can't imagine how happy it makes me having you here."

When the food arrived, they ate in companionable silence, then watched Kenji Mizoguchi's *The Life of Oharu*, the film Yuke had been writing about. Mara was greatly moved by this story of a woman struggling against patriarchal oppression in seventeenth century Japan, and identified with its tragic heroine. When the film finished, Yuke discussed her ideas for the piece she was preparing, and Mara was stunned by their brilliance. It seemed unfair that the Melissa Valance novels made so much money, while Yuke's more intellectually strenuous labours of love barely covered her expenses. Yuke never actually said so, but this was obviously the reason she'd not yet moved to the more expensive area in which Mara lived. Mara knew Yuke was too proud to accept money, but she longed to help her escape from East Finchley. She was tempted to tell Yuke about the news reports concerning Julie's death and the absurd message from Tyner, but she'd managed to go for several hours without thinking of the Hunt, and didn't want to introduce a subject which would again make her confront that horror. In a way, Tyner's email had actually helped, allowing her to temper the hatred which threatened to overwhelm her with a dash of contempt.

But there was a related matter she needed to discuss with Yuke, and when they were in bed that evening, Mara tentatively broached it by showing Yuke the jar of Hunex. "I've been using this," she said as casually as possible, "since Monday. It helps a lot. Strangely enough, I didn't feel any pain during the weekend. When you were staying over." Yuke looked embarrassed. Mara kissed her gently, and whispered the words "Thank you" in her ear, adding, "You must have been in agony."

"It wasn't that bad. It made me feel good knowing I was helping you."

"Can you control it? When I took the pain from your hand, it was completely involuntary."

"I'd never tried doing anything like this before. But I think I could control it. I wouldn't have been able to do it unless I'd wanted to. It's the same with your dreams. I don't actively seek them out, but if I wanted them to disappear, to go back into your head, I know they would." Yuke laughed, perceiving the craziness of what she was saying. "Oh Mara, what's happening to us?"

"I don't know. But I'm sure it's something good. Something important."

They both slept peacefully that night, and when Mara left the following morning, she felt rejuvenated. Even her customary sadness upon departing from Yuke was eased by the knowledge they'd be together again the following day.

When she returned home, Mara found an email from Kate Mackendrick. Kate thanked Mara for everything she'd done during the Hunt, and mentioned that if she ever made it to Glasgow, she'd be welcome to stay with her. Mara responded with a similar message offering Kate accommodation in London. She greatly admired this woman, who had sailed through the Hunt without so much as a scratch and effortlessly humiliated her would-be tormentor.

Mara believed she was finally ready to do some serious work on *A Kill is Just a Kill*, but the novel continued to progress sluggishly, and when she looked back over the completed sections on Friday morning, she was dismayed to find them as dull to read as they were to write. She had just made the decision to scrap what she'd done so far and start again when the doorbell rang. Standing outside was a postman, though happily not the one who had delivered her induction notice. He handed her an envelope without saying a word, not even "banooseferoo.'"As Mara looked at it, her heart sank, for the 'Department of Corrections' logo was stamped on the front. After placing her thumb on the postman's scanner, she slammed the door, tore open the envelope, and read the letter it contained.

"To Mara Gorki.

Following a complaint, supported by photographic evidence, from a member of the public, you have been found guilty of appearing out of uniform in a public place on March 26th of this year.

As this is a second offence, you have been sentenced to twenty strokes of the cane.

You are hereby ordered to present yourself at Camden Punishment Centre on April 13th at three p.m., at which time the sentence will be carried out.

Paul Booth
Department of Corrections.

Mara felt like punching the wall. So Tyner had carried out his idiotic threat! And the DoC had taken him seriously! April 13th was the following Friday, and Mara already had an appointment with her lawyer scheduled for Monday. Perhaps Madeleine could file an appeal on her behalf. The whole thing seemed ridiculous, but she needed to mentally prepare herself for more punishment. She went to the bathroom, lowered her jeans and looked at her buttocks in the mirror. The marks from the Hunt barely seemed to have faded, and she still needed to apply the cream she'd been prescribed: the last thing she wanted was another caning.

As soon as Yuke arrived, Mara showed her the letter, as well as Tyner's email. She didn't want there to be any secrets between them. Yuke seemed optimistic about the appeal, but Mara could tell she was upset. For the next few days, Mara tried pushing the sentence to the back of her mind, telling herself she'd been subjected to so much physical abuse lately that twenty strokes of the cane would be almost insignificant. She was only partially successful. It was a shame, because otherwise the weekend turned out to be wonderful. Yuke gave Mara an old paperback of a novel called *Lilith* by J. R. Salamanca, insisting she'd love it. It was the kind of poetically evocative Americana Mara adored, and the two women spent more than an hour reading out random passages to each other. It was usually Mara who introduced Yuke to rare books, and Yuke who introduced Mara to obscure films, but this perfect gift suggested they were exchanging roles and personalities, merging into a single entity. Maybe this was what their dreamcatching and painsharing had been leading towards. Mara suspected that the point at which she ended and Yuke began was gradually being obscured. She thought back to something Julie had said about loss of identity and individuality, and how death was the ultimate loss of individuality. Perhaps her identity was being submerged in Yuke's, but it certainly didn't feel like a loss. On the contrary, it was as if she were being expanded. When she was with Yuke, she believed herself capable of anything.

On Sunday morning, Mara read Yuke some of the news reports relating to Julie that had appeared over the last few days, and Yuke suggested trying to find out more about Robert Price. Predictably, the name was a familiar one. Wikipedia alone listed more than a dozen Robert or Bob Prices, including an American theologian, an eighteenth century judge, and a seventeenth century bishop. But by using Google Images, Mara managed to locate the creature she still thought of as Let's-Make-a-Deal. It turned out he was an examiner at the British Board of Film Classification, the UK's state censor board for films and DVDs. The BBFC's website included a profile of Price, together with a photo of him smiling pleasantly, and quoted him as saying, "I joined the BBFC because I admired its efforts to stem the tide of cinematic filth. In recent years, films that portray homosexuality as a normal activity and plumb the depths of depravity have been widely seen in America, Asia and Europe. I am proud to live in a country where such things are unacceptable." Mara wondered what Price's colleagues would have thought if they'd seen this depravity-hating censor during the Hunt. Perhaps they wouldn't have been shocked at all. The Hunt was legal, and Price associated depravity with homosexuality, not torturing young women to death. Yuke was appalled, but not surprised. She had friends who used to run arthouse DVD labels, but were forced out of business because they couldn't afford to pay the BBFC's 'certification' fees. According to her, film examiners, who charged by the minute, and literature examiners, who charged by the word, made more money than most directors and writers. Mara wasn't surprised either. In 1821, Heinrich Heine wrote a play entitled *Almansor*, which contained the line, "Where they burn books, they will ultimately burn people also." It seemed obvious to Mara that a society which privileged censorship over art would end up creating something like the Hunt. She thought of Julie singing her beautiful song, and imagined Price censoring his daily quota of films. She recalled hearing of a censor in ancient Rome who began a speech with the words, "Gentlemen, were we ever to find a means to live without women, thereupon unto us should true happiness be known." The battle lines were drawn with stark clarity: creativity against suppression, freedom against control, femininity against masculinity, Life against Death. At the moment, Death seemed to be winning.

CHAPTER 20

When Mara walked into Madeleine's office on Monday morning, the lawyer greeted her with an affectionate embrace. "I'm so glad to see you," she said. "I heard somebody had died during the Hunt, and my first thought was that it could have been you."

"That's partly what I wanted to talk about," said Mara as she sat in the chair opposite Madeleine's desk. "But something else has come up." Mara showed Madeleine the letter she'd received, and explained the story behind it, mentioning that she was especially eager to avoid a caning, since there was already a danger of permanent scarring.

After reading the letter, Madeleine said, "This Stephen Tyner could get into trouble for trying to blackmail you, but I suspect he has his reasons. If your scars are still visible six months after the Hunt, you could sue him. This way, he can claim they were caused by your judicial punishment. I think we have solid grounds for an appeal, but it wouldn't surprise me if Tyner turns up to give evidence. That shouldn't make much difference, though. Leave it with me. What was the other thing you wanted to discuss?"

"That's more serious."

During the next thirty minutes, Mara told Madeleine everything she recalled about Robert Price: about the deal he'd attempted to make with Mara, and the way he'd forced her to collaborate in Julie's torture. By the time Mara had finished, the lawyer's face was pale. After a long silence, Madeleine said, "Price can't be allowed to get away with this. Are you willing to repeat what you've just told me in court?"

Mara didn't hesitate before saying, "Yes."

Madeleine made a note in her diary. "I'll get in touch with the family's lawyer. You'll need to make a statement at some point."

"Just try and stop me," said Mara, adding, "Though the Weiszs may not want anything to do with me. I broke the news of Julie's death to them, and they asked me to leave them alone. It was obviously because they couldn't accept what I was saying, but don't be surprised if they'd prefer me not to be involved."

———

Madeleine phoned Mara the following day to inform her that the appeal would take place on Friday at one-thirty. "It'll be heard at Camden Punishment Centre, and if it isn't successful, you'll receive the caning more or less immediately. At least that way you won't have to wait around. And I'm reasonably certain of a positive outcome."

"Any news about the Weiszs?"

"I've written to Aaron Rosenbaum. Hopefully, I'll hear from him soon. One more thing. Could you send me the email you received from Tyner?"

As soon as Madeleine hung up, Mara forwarded the email. Now there was nothing to do but wait. Wait and resume work on a novel stubbornly refusing to flow. Perhaps when the appeal was over and, one way or another, she didn't have the threat of another flogging hanging over her, she'd be able to concentrate on her writing. But then there would be the painful task of reconnecting with the Weiszs, and whatever followed from that. It seemed the Hunt would be casting its shadow over her for some time to come.

———

The night prior to her appeal, Mara had trouble sleeping. She lay awake, trying to prepare herself for the ordeal she believed was inevitable. Madeleine had sounded confident, but Mara did not share her optimism. She now knew a great deal about how the system worked. And she felt afraid. Which was exactly the way she was meant to feel. Fear was the oil that kept the gears of oppression turning. Far more than pain or humiliation, fear was what Britain's rulers wanted the country's female inhabitants to become familiar with. Fear usually kept women in line, and should they be caught breaking the law, their anxiety while waiting for a sentence to be carried out was itself part of the punishment. This was surely why 'criminals' were informed at least a week in advance of the date on which they'd be caned, or have one of their limbs amputated. The fear Mara was now experiencing demonstrated just how skilled the authorities were at manipulation. They were playing her like a harp. Mara thought of Tyner, who seemed to thrive on her terror. He was the perfect representative of malinism, the living embodiment of an ideology dependent upon the subjugation of women and the suppression of femininity. And if Mara regarded her forthcoming appeal as futile, she was even more pessimistic about the chances of Price being made to pay for Julie's murder. Defeating Price would mean defeating the regime responsible for his actions, and that was not going to happen.

Mara fell asleep just after seven a.m., and woke around eleven. She took a shower and checked to see how much Hunex she had left. The jar was still half full. She hadn't used the cream in almost four days, but strongly suspected she'd need it later that afternoon. Unable to eat anything, she made some coffee and watched her bedside clock as it counted down the minutes to twelve-fifteen, at which time she put on her uniform and headed for Camden.

The punishment centre looked much as she remembered it from her previous visit. It was a remarkably anonymous building, and one would never have guessed what went on inside. She'd arrived ten minutes early, but Madeleine was already standing outside, holding an impressive-looking briefcase. Her professional demeanour filled Mara with confidence. They shook hands - embraces would have been out of place here - and Madeleine suggested they wait a few minutes before going inside. "I'd rather not be in there any longer than I have to. I was heavily involved with the protest movement during the '40s - that's how I got to know your parents - and it was these places that killed it off. Back then, the police would arrest anyone taking part in demonstrations, but all they could do was lock us up for a few days, a week or two at most. With the women's prisons full of protesters, they became meeting places for radicals. We'd sit in our cells planning the next march. It was one big party. But then the courts began sending us to punishment centres. I had to report for a caning once, and as soon as I felt the first stroke, I knew the party was over. Most of us abandoned the cause, or channelled our anger in another direction. That's why I became a lawyer. Later on, the amputations started. When the Hunt was introduced, not a single person dared publicly protest, though I suppose anger about the February 16th bombings might have had something to do with that. Nobody wanted to be perceived as a feminist."

Mara thought for a moment, then said, "There's something you should know."

She spent the next few minutes telling Madeleine about Mary Green's letter, and what it implied. When Mara had finished, Madeleine looked around carefully to make sure nobody was listening. "Have you mentioned this to anyone else?" she asked quietly.

"Only Yuke."

"I think it would be better if you kept this to yourself. At least for now. If what you've said is true, and I don't doubt that it is, you could end up making some very powerful enemies." Looking at her watch, Madeleine said, "We'd better go in."

They walked through the punishment centre's door, and Madeleine handed an official document to the receptionist, who gave her the most incongruous smile imaginable and said, "Somebody will be down to collect you shortly." They sat in the waiting area, which was already occupied by five other women, one of whom appeared to be in her fifties. Mara couldn't help thinking how humiliating it must be for someone of that age to receive corporal punishment. The woman seemed vaguely familiar, and after searching her memory, Mara realised she was the spitting image of Mary Green. Could it actually be her? Mara was wondering if she should say something when a man in a dark suit strode through the front door and proceeded to a nearby elevator. Madeleine leaned over and whispered, "That's Judge Birney. He'll be hearing your appeal. I don't know him, but he has a reputation for being fair."

The door opened again almost immediately, and Mara was disgusted to see Tyner walk in and approach the receptionist, who indicated he should take a seat. He sat as far away from Mara as possible, but when he inadvertently caught her eye, he smiled and waved, as if they were old friends. Mara did not return the wave. "That's Tyner," she whispered to Madeleine.

"I thought he'd be here," Madeleine whispered back. "I read his email, and I gather we're not exactly dealing with the next Oscar Wilde. It's just possible that...well, let's see how fair this judge is."

Mara noticed Tyner trying to start a conversation with a young woman sitting near him; the woman stood up and moved to a different chair. As she did this, a man with a clipboard appeared from a room behind the receptionist's desk. After reading out the names Madeleine Danes, Mara Gorki and Stephen Tyner, he said, "Please follow me," in a voice that was barely audible. He led his charges to the elevator, and once they were inside, Madeleine deliberately positioned herself between Mara and Tyner. Mara felt grateful for this: she didn't want to stand any closer to her tormentor - and now accuser - than necessary.

When they arrived at the top floor, Clipboard Man showed them into a small room and silently vanished, shutting the door behind him. The room was bare except for a conference table which might have accommodated eight people. Judge Birney was already seated, poring over some documents. "Sit down," he said brusquely. Madeleine waited until Tyner had taken a seat on the left of the table, leaving several empty spaces between himself and the Judge. Placing her briefcase on the table, she sat on the Judge's immediate right, indicating that Mara should sit next to her.

Consulting one of the papers before him, the Judge said, "Mara Gorki?"

"Here, Your Honour," replied Mara, who had read enough courtroom thrillers to know the correct response.

"Madeleine Danes?"

"Here, Your Honour."

"Stephen Tyner?"

Tyner answered with a grunt.

The Judge narrowed his eyes, then looked up and said, "I am here to consider Miss Gorki's appeal against a sentence imposed upon her for appearing out of uniform in a public place. Miss Danes, you may begin."

Mara expected Madeleine to stand up, but she merely leaned back in her chair and addressed her remarks to the Judge. "My client stands accused of appearing out of uniform in a public place on March 26th. Your Honour will note that on this date, my client was participating in a Hunt. She had hidden in an abandoned apartment, and changed into the clothes she found there, as she believed they would permit her greater freedom of movement should she need to run from a Hunter. Hunt rules explicitly state that female participants may take whatever evasive action they feel is necessary to avoid capture."

The Judge interrupted her. "Hunt rules also explicitly state that female participants are to wear full uniform."

The Judge's remark hit Mara like a hammer blow, but Madeleine didn't miss a beat. "I believe Your Honour is referring to the induction letter which does indeed instruct participants to wear full uniform. But it is our contention that this applies solely to the journey to and from the stadium. The Female Uniform Act of 2045 states that women participating in sporting events in places dedicated to such activities may wear clothing appropriate for the particular sport. Hunt rules specifically refer to the place in which the Hunt occurs as a stadium, which implies a place dedicated to a sporting event. In any case, the stadium cannot be regarded as a public place, as it is consists of a walled off area hosting a private function to which members of the general public are not admitted. Furthermore, Miss Gorki was only wearing non-uniform clothes while occupying an abandoned apartment. She did not step outside this apartment until forced to do so by Mr. Tyner, who did not give her the opportunity to change back into her uniform.' As she said this, Madeleine removed from her briefcase a printout of the photo taken by Tyner. 'If you look at this photo carefully, Your Honour, you will see that Miss Gorki is wearing the collar which had been locked on her by Mr. Tyner, and at this point was clearly acting under Mr. Tyner's direction. This is the basis on which we are appealing the court's decision."

The Judge turned towards Tyner and said, "Mr. Tyner, what is your response?"

Tyner sat up, shuffling uncomfortably in his seat, and said, "I used a body heat detector to locate Miss Gorki in a building where she was, like, hiding. She tried to escape by climbing onto the roof, and when I pursued her up there, I noticed she was out of uniform. She told me her uniform was in the apartment where she'd been hiding, so I went to get it. I then instructed Miss Gorki to proceed to the Hunters' block, where…"

"Where was the uniform at this point?" interjected the Judge.

"In my backpack."

"Did you instruct Miss Gorki to put it on?"

"No. If she'd, like, asked me for permission to change into the uniform, I would given it to her. But she didn't ask."

"By the time you had entered the apartment and collected the uniform, was Miss Gorki wearing your collar?"

"Yes, Your Honour."

"So we would assume, would we not, that Miss Gorki was not acting of her own free will, but rather under your orders."

"Yes, I suppose that's true. But I never, like, told her to take the uniform off."

"As far as you are aware, did Miss Gorki appear outside the apartment without her uniform before you pursued her onto the roof?"

"I didn't see her before that, so I don't know."

The Judge grimaced. "I'll repeat the question. As far as you are aware, did Miss Gorki appear outside the apartment without her uniform before you pursued her onto the roof?"

Tyner seemed to be searching for an answer on the floor. "Yes or no, Mr. Tyner?" said the Judge in an exasperated voice.

"No," admitted Tyner with obvious reluctance.

"And do you have any specific response to Miss Danes' appeal?"

"Specific response?" asked Tyner, as if the Judge were speaking Greek.

"Is there any part of the appeal you disagree with?"

"Well, yes."

"Which part?"

"All of it."

"And exactly why do you disagree with all of it?"

Tyner was looking extremely uncomfortable. This clearly wasn't what he'd been expecting. "Well, I…I just think it's wrong."

The expression on the Judge's face left no doubt that he'd finally had enough. Dismissing Tyner with a wave of the hand, he turned towards Mara, and for the first time addressed her directly. "Miss Gorki. Rules are meant to be obeyed, and I would not want to make a decision that might set a precedent. But given the specific circumstances under which you came to be out of uniform, I have decided to rule in your favour. Your appeal is granted, and the sentence cancelled."

Mara almost jumped out of her chair with joy. She glanced at Madeleine, expecting her to look equally pleased, but the lawyer's mouth was set in a grim line. Madeleine removed a piece of paper from her briefcase and passed it to the Judge. "I would like to draw Your Honour's attention to this printout of an email sent by Mr. Tyner to my client on April 2nd, in particular the passage I have highlighted in yellow. It's rather hard to read, as Mr. Tyner's spelling, grammar and punctuation leave a great deal to be desired, but I think the general meaning is clear enough."

The Judge examined the paper, then passed it to Tyner, asking, "Mr. Tyner, did you write and send this email?"

Tyner stared, slack-jawed, at the printout, obviously wondering if he could get away with denying it, then nodded his head and said, "Yes, Your Honour."

The Judge took the paper back and looked at it again, saying, "This is extremely difficult to make sense of, but I believe it says 'I know I said I would report you for being out of uniform, but if you were willing to play with me some more, I would forget about the whole thing.' Mr. Tyner, what exactly did you mean by 'play with me some more'?"

Tyner obviously wished a hole would open up and swallow him. "Well, I meant we could do some of the things we did during the Hunt."

"What things exactly?"

"Things...we did."

"Be specific. What things?"

"Well, we used, like, the cane and the whip...um...needles."

"And what did you do with the needles?"

"I...pierced Miss Gorki's nipples. Which...which is one of the things I was permitted to do."

"I see. And you thought Miss Gorki might volunteer to have her nipples pierced again?"

Tyner leaned forward, and tried talking to the Judge in what he seemingly regarded as a man-to-man way. "You see, Your Honour, women like being dominated by men. I thought Mara…I mean Miss Gorki, secretly enjoyed what we did together, and would welcome the opportunity to do some more."

"Then why did you try to blackmail her?"

"I didn't!"

The Judge held up the sheet of paper. "It says so right here. You told Miss Gorki that if she were willing to play with you, you would forget about reporting her for being out of uniform."

And at long last, it occurred to Tyner that a hole had indeed opened up and swallowed him, and he was digging it deeper with every word. Sitting up straight, he looked at the wall opposite and declared, "I'm not saying anything else until I see a lawyer."

The Judge could barely conceal his contempt. "I suggest you see that lawyer very soon, Mr. Tyner, since I intend to have you prosecuted for attempted blackmail, and I will recommend you receive a severe judicial caning. Now if there's nothing further to discuss, you may all leave."

Mara did not even try to hide the smile which had spread over her face as she listened to this conversation. Madeleine maintained a facade of disinterest until they were back in the corridor, at which point she grinned and said, "That went even better than expected."

As they waited for the elevator, Tyner walked up and leaned against a wall. He clearly didn't want to be anywhere near these women, but recent events had so disoriented him that he didn't have the energy to conceal himself until they'd gone. When the elevator door opened, Mara moved aside and made a mock bow to Tyner, repeating the gesture he'd used during the Hunt. Tyner silently entered the elevator, and Mara followed, this time making sure she stood next to him. Madeleine, who was facing both of them, looked amused. As the door closed, Mara turned to Tyner and said, "Don't be afraid of this judicial caning. Think of it as an opportunity to, like, test your pain threshold. You may be reluctant to admit it, but I'm sure you'll be turned on. You're going to learn a few things about yourself that might, like, surprise you. The fact you've absolutely no choice is precisely what will make this experience such an exciting one. I know you don't, like, like safe words, so it won't bother you that there aren't any. Just think of the man who canes you as your guide." This last comment was made to Tyner's retreating back as he ran from the elevator, which had just reached the ground floor, and tore out of the building. Mara and Madeleine collapsed in a fit of helpless laughter. All this was observed with bemusement by the receptionist, who wasn't used to seeing running men and laughing women in the punishment centre.

"My God," gasped Madeleine, "was that really the kind of shit he said to you?"

"Almost verbatim," replied Mara, adding, "Thank you so much for this. I don't know what I'd have done without you."

"You'd have found another lawyer who was equally good. Anyway, we women have to look out for each other. Because nobody else will."

Mara nodded, then said, "Though I was impressed by that Judge. Sometimes I think there might be men who are on our side. I feel almost hopeful about the future."

Madeleine smiled sweetly and said, "Speaking of which, I'm going to be meeting with Aaron Rosenbaum on Monday. I'll let you know what he says."

Madeleine returned to her office, and Mara, her step lighter than it had been for weeks, caught the tube, first texting a message to Yuke: "Appeal granted. No caning. At least for me. I'll tell you everything tonight." As she took her seat on the train, she remembered the middle-aged woman in the punishment centre. Only now did she realise there was something distinctly odd about this encounter. She'd been struck by the woman's resemblance to Mary Green. But Mara had never seen Mary Green, had never even read a description of her, had absolutely no way of knowing what she looked like. What on Earth could have been going through her mind?

When Yuke arrived at the apartment that evening, she listened open-mouthed as Mara recounted the story of Tyner's grilling by the Judge. They decided to send out a group email inviting their friends, Madeleine included, to meet them for a celebration at the Benugo Bar on Saturday. Mara reserved The Drawing Room, a small cocktail bar concealed behind the lounge area, and spent several hours surrounded by people she loved.

She even felt confident enough to kiss Yuke on the lips: they were in a semi-public area, but the only stranger was a female bartender, who winked at them. Before departing, Madeleine embraced Yuke and said, "Take good care of Mara. She's a very special person." Any doubts the lawyer might still have had about the nature of Mara's relationship with Yuke did not survive the evening.

CHAPTER 21

The investigation into Julie Weisz's death proceeded with remarkable speed. At the family's request, a second postmortem was carried out on April 20th by an independent coroner, who concluded Julie had died of exhaustion, shock, and cardiac arrest following days of sustained torture. Soon after this, Madeleine set up a meeting between Mara and Aaron Rosenbaum. It was Aaron who informed Mara that Julie's boyfriend, himself a talented musician and songwriter, had committed suicide. So two young lives full of potential had been cut short because of Price's sadistic urges. Mara told Aaron everything she knew about Julie's death, and he took the responsibility of passing this information on to the girl's parents. When Mara was officially introduced to the Weiszs, they literally got down on their knees and begged her to forgive them for their behaviour outside the stadium. After that, they treated her as if she were Julie reincarnated. But the more affection they lavished on Mara, the worse she felt. She knew enough about psychoanalysis to be familiar with the concept of survivor's guilt, but realising she was exhibiting the classic symptoms of a widely recognised condition didn't help. She kept going over the many things she could have done differently, things that might have changed the fatal outcome. If only she'd taken Price up on his offer, or chosen a different hiding place, or stopped Julie from going out to use the vending machine, or not told Tyner that Julie was her friend. That last mistake particularly haunted her, because it was so pointless. How could she have been stupid enough to think somebody as detached from normal emotions as Tyner would fail to exploit something so pathetically sentimental as one human being's concern for another?

A very un-Melissa Valance-like private detective named Ray Walcott was hired by the family, though with nobody except Mara willing to talk to him, his investigation ran into a wall. But both Aaron and Madeleine believed Mara's testimony and the results of the second postmortem were enough to justify a trial. They presented their evidence to the Director of Public Prosecutions, making it clear that if Robert Price was not prosecuted, they would take the case to the European court. The DPP had little choice but to schedule a trial for late June. During the following weeks, Walcott discovered that pathologist Dr. Frederick Letap was a notorious incompetent who tended to be called in whenever somebody wanted to muddy the waters. He'd recently conducted a postmortem on a woman who'd been beaten to death by two police officers for the crime of talking back to them. Letap claimed the victim had died of a drug-related illness, and insisted he could find no signs of violence, even though she was covered in bruises, her left arm broken, and her skull fractured. Letap subsequently mislaid the sample he'd taken of the victim's blood, and despite two subsequent postmortems which concluded the woman had died due to a sustained assault, the accused officers were found not guilty. The authorities clearly expected the same thing to happen if Price ever came to trial, but Aaron hoped to expose Letap in front of the jury.

The trial began on June 27th. Newspaper editors had made an unspoken pact not to publicise the Weiszs' quest for justice, but they could hardly ignore a prominent murder trial. Their approach, predictably, was to present Price as an innocent victim of circumstance persecuted by a couple whose grief had driven them insane. When Price took the stand on June 29th, the sympathy for him emanating from the public gallery was almost palpable. Julie, who attended every day of the trial, barely recognised him. He'd apparently spent quality time with a good drama coach. His stooped posture evoked memories of Charles Laughton in *The Hunchback of Notre Dame*, and his eyes were constantly directed upward, as if begging a merciful God to take pity on him in his time of need. His voice was gentle, and his hands frequently clasped, as if in prayer. He'd even taken to using a walking stick. Aaron was intensely aware of how negatively the jury responded whenever he subjected Price to tough questioning. As he told the Weiszs, "The best we can hope for is to expose the sadistic cruelty of the Hunt, because the jury will never send this man to prison." As part of this strategy, Aaron asked Price to read the section of the Hunt pamphlet outlining how Hunters were permitted to treat their victims. Although several members of the all-male jury were plainly unsettled by this account of state-sanctioned torture, they refused to accept that a man like Price, a man any girl would be happy to take home to mother, could do such things.

But Aaron believed he had an ace up his sleeve. The country's leading pathologist had conducted a third postmortem on May 7th, and prepared a detailed report describing precisely how the wounds on Julie's body had been caused. Aaron expected Price to deny having done anything to Julie. His plan was to bring out the undeniable forensic evidence and break Price down, forcing him to admit how he'd made his victim suffer. But Price had access to some expensive legal talent, and they'd prepared an almost perfect defence. When Aaron asked how he'd treated Julie, Price had his story well rehearsed, and wouldn't budge from it. He claimed to have entered the Hunt because he approved of the way it deterred terrorists, and wanted to show his support: but he hadn't planned on actually doing anything except a little light spanking, and not even that if the person he caught wasn't willing. But, to his horror, Julie turned out to be an extreme masochist. Yes, he'd pierced her nipples, attached a clamp to her clitoris, used electricity on her genitalia, flogged her until she was covered in blood and her skin raw, raped her repeatedly, both vaginally and anally. But she'd begged him to do all these things. She hadn't even wanted to sleep in a bed, instead demanding he strap her to the wooden horse, or lock her in the cage, or suspend her from the ceiling by her breasts, and leave her in these positions overnight. He'd pleaded with her to let him rest, but she'd merely laughed, called him names, and insisted he continue.

With Price admitting to having done everything the pathologist's report irrefutably proved he'd done, evidence became of secondary importance. All that remained was to demonstrate the sheer implausibility of Price's narrative. Why, asked Aaron, had Julie's parents and friends never noticed these masochistic tendencies? Perhaps she was ashamed of them, suggested Price in a reasonable tone, and tried to keep them secret. Or perhaps participating in the Hunt had unleashed desires Julie never knew she had.

Aaron's response was to put Mara on the stand and have her tell the jury what she'd observed. Mara calmly recounted how Price had approached her during the initial meeting and offered to go easy on her if she surrendered to him. And she described, detail by detail, what happened when Price brought Julie to Tyner's playroom. At least three of the jurymen gasped when Mara quoted Price as saying, "I intend to make sure this vile cunt remembers tonight for the rest of her life." Even Price expressed shock and disbelief. When he once again took the stand, he was willing to admit that much of what Mara said was true. He had brought Julie to Tyner's apartment and coerced Mara into torturing her. But, he insisted, it was all Julie's idea. She'd wanted to play a practical joke on her friend. Julie had indeed appeared to be terrified, but that was all part of the act. She'd planned to let Mara in on the joke when they were released the following day. But Price denied having said anything to Mara at the meeting, except that he hoped she'd enjoy the Hunt. "She looked a bit nervous," he recalled, "and I wanted to cheer her up." And he'd certainly not said that terrible thing in the playroom. Shaking his head in sadness, he reluctantly admitted that Mara seemed to be a bit of a fantasist. "Mr. Tyner told me she spent an entire evening ranting about one of her pet conspiracy theories. Apparently, she believes the 2059 bombings were carried out by the government." The jury chuckled at this, and Price smiled, like a nightclub comedian whose latest joke has been well received.

And that was pretty much the end of the case for the prosecution. Aaron wanted to introduce evidence of Dr. Letap's incompetence, but the Judge ruled it inadmissible. Tyner had been subpoenaed, but was no longer resident in the U.K.. When Mara last saw him, he'd been running from the Camden Punishment Centre, and it seemed he hadn't stopped until reaching France. The opportunity to test his pain threshold apparently held little appeal.

The defence focused on the fact that Price had done nothing illegal during the Hunt. The one thing he could be accused of was using excessive force, and hadn't he explained that Miss Weisz nagged away at him until, in order to satisfy her perverse desires, he'd been coerced into acting against his better judgement?

Dr. Roberts was then brought to the stand. He'd examined Miss Weisz every day, he insisted, and seen nothing to suggest her health was being endangered. She died, he pointed out, after his final examination, so what happened during her final hours was beyond his control. He did recall her begging him to put an end to her agony, but his psychiatric training enabled him to perceive that these pleas were actually Miss Weisz's way of furthering her masochistic agenda, allowing her to view herself as the helpless victim she so longed to be.

When Mara returned to the stand, all the defence lawyer wanted to discuss was her theory concerning the 2059 bombings. Madeleine had suggested she keep quiet about her discovery, but she'd forgotten having already mentioned it to Tyner. The cat was now out of the bag, and Mara decided truth would be the best weapon to use against Price's lies. She told of how she'd come across Mary Green's letter, which revealed that, after leaving Kilburn's homeless alone for over a decade, the police had started clearing them out of the area one week before the supposed terrorist attack took place. Turning to the jury, Mara said, "Decide for yourselves if this was nothing more than a coincidence." Price's lawyer looked at the jury, twisting his face and shaking his head in a manner which suggested they should all pretend to believe Mara, as she might become violent if contradicted. Mara wasn't so sure the jurymen saw things this way: some of them were visibly disturbed.

But in the end, it made no difference. The defence pointed out that although certain individuals disagreed with Dr. Letap, he was nonetheless the first person to examine the corpse, and his opinions thus carried more weight than those of subsequent pathologists. As had been intended all along, Letap so confused the issue that there was no way for the jury to definitively conclude Julie hadn't died of natural causes. They declared Price not guilty.

The press response was unanimously favourable. "Justice Prevails" read the **Daily Male**'s headline, pages two and three being entirely dedicated to coverage of the trial. Needless to say, these 'objective' news reports were slanted to make the prosecution's claims seem absurd. Mara, who was depicted as a mad conspiracy theorist, wept when she read the articles. She'd desperately wanted Price to face justice, yet he'd ended up being exonerated, while Julie, who should have been known as a talented singer and songwriter, would be remembered as a masochist responsible for her own death.

Yet once she'd gone through all the reports in detail, she began to see a positive side. For there, on the state-approved Internet and in the cold light of print, were full details about what took place during a Hunt. Perhaps this would open people's eyes and make them acknowledge what was going on. When Germany's post-Nazi youth asked how their parents could have stood by while millions of Jews were murdered, the older generation claimed not to have known what was happening. The people of Great Britain could no longer make such a claim, for all the information they needed could be found in the newspapers. Even Mara's theory about the 2059 bombings was there: ridiculed, yes - talk show hosts had even started telling Mara Gorki jokes - but openly expressed in a way that would surely make at least some people have second thoughts about the Brave New World in which they lived. Right now, all this didn't seem like much. But what was it Mary Green had written? "I feel confident that this small flame can be fanned into a blaze which will sweep away the misogyny and injustice being foisted on this country's citizens."

CHAPTER 22

While searching for articles on the trial, Mara had come across a *Daily Male* editorial which, unusually for this newspaper, touched on literary matters.

"*Double or Nothing*, the latest novel by Jason Amis, has sparked a controversy due to the fact that certain sections have been removed by order of the British Board of Fiction Classification, even though the book was given an Unsuitable for Women rating. Mr. Amis and his admirers argue that adult males should be permitted to read whatever they wish, and that the book should have been published uncut. This is a viewpoint with which we have some sympathy. But we feel obliged to point out that although it might be illegal to sell a UFW-rated book to a woman, once that book is taken into the home, it can be read by anyone who picks it up. This is why the versions of UFW-rated films released on DVD are more heavily censored than those screened theatrically. We can be reasonably certain that women will not view UFW films in cinemas, but controls are inevitably laxer in the domestic sphere, and careless husbands frequently neglect to place UFW discs under lock and key. Some men don't even see anything wrong with allowing their wives access to inappropriate books and films. When making a classification decision, the BBFC's filmic branch is obliged to consider the question, 'Is this work suitable for viewing in the home?' while the board's literary branch is obliged to consider the question, 'Is this a book that you would wish your wife or your servants to read?' Nobody would claim that *Double or Nothing* is suitable for women, even in its present form. But the BBFC, mindful of their statutory obligations, have purged those sections - involving women pursuing their own sexual agendas - which would prove especially damaging to female readers. Thanks to the publisher, we have been able to sample the passages in question, and can unequivocally state that we would not want to live in a country where women could read such material. The BBFC was created to maintain a balance between the rights of men to be entertained, and the needs of women to be protected. In our opinion, they are doing an excellent job."

The knowledge that Julie's murderer was a BBFC examiner made Mara especially attentive to information about this organisation, and the editorial greatly disturbed her, though more because of what it left out than what it included. The *Daily Male*'s editor evidently didn't realise how easy it was for women to obtain uncensored books and DVDs. What would he have said if he'd known that the notorious Mara Gorki had recently been able to buy *The Scum Manifesto* at a shop in central London? Reading and film viewing had become such marginal activities that politicians hadn't seen much point in passing legislation making it illegal for women to purchase uncertified material second hand or through import websites. But a tabloid campaign might make them change their minds. More books were receiving UFW-ratings lately, and the ratings were being taken more seriously. While shopping for groceries in her local supermarket a few weeks after the trial, Mara had come across a small display of paperbacks which included a new novel she was interested in. It was rated UFW, but Mara had decided to try buying it anyway, hoping the man behind the check-out counter would be too busy to notice the certificate. If he did notice, she assumed he'd simply refuse to sell her the book. But upon seeing the UFW stamp, the man had grabbed Mara's arm, leaving the rest of her shopping sitting on the conveyor belt, and taken her to see the store's manager, who offered her a choice between being reported to the police, or receiving a dozen blows across her palms with a heavy ruler he kept in his office for just such a purpose. Desperate to avoid another punishment centre appointment, Mara had opted for the ruler, but her hands had swelled up so badly as a result of the beating that she'd been unable to write for three days. She'd subsequently ordered the novel online, but such sources of supply could be outlawed at the stroke of a ministerial pen. Mara dreaded the day when her choice of reading material would be limited to those sanitised texts considered suitable for female consumption. She recalled Ray Bradbury's *Fahrenheit 451*, in which books were banned and firemen burned hidden collections. Could something like that happen here? Could somebody come into her home and confiscate her library? For Mara, a life without books would hardly be worth living. And what about her work? How long could she reasonably expect to get away with turning out novels which criticised the state, even if they were only published abroad? She had become a public figure, and could no longer hide behind a mask of obscurity.

Now more than ever, it seemed important to seek out openly articulated hints of dissatisfaction, pockets of organised resistance, flames that could be fanned. Mara kept a close eye on Internet boards which tended to attract female contributors, and soon noticed signs of online activism. Messages had to be carefully phrased: there were no demands for radical change, only hints that essentially admirable institutions might be improved by minor reforms, but the tide did seem to be turning. Mara came across threads pointing out the need for greater medical supervision during the Hunt, and suggesting abortions be permitted in cases involving rape. She cautiously started a thread of her own urging people to write their MPs requesting women be given the option of wearing trousers during the cold winter months. Mara knew this campaign had little chance of success, but it seemed a point worth making, and she was gratified by the enthusiastic responses her post attracted. "Great idea!" read one. "If we can't wear trousers in the winter, how about at least allowing us thicker tights?" Politicians would appear unreasonable when they refused to implement even such mild proposals, and the subsequent perception of unfairness might generate sympathy for progressive causes. But, at least so far, nobody had dared write anything about relaxing the laws against homosexuality. Anyone who openly advocated such a thing might find their private lives being investigated, and the supposedly platonic nature of Mara's friendship with Yuke would not withstand scrutiny.

Due to her involvement with the Price trial, Mara frequently received emails from women who had been conscripted and were seeking practical advice. Remembering Claire's willingness to share painful memories with a stranger, Mara found time for everyone who needed her. She assumed the Hunters would start using a different tracking method now their old one had been exposed, so the only suggestion she could make to the terrified draftees who consulted her was that they remain especially alert during the initial meeting. She never mentioned Apartment 1708. Tyner had surely reported the place, so it would most likely have been cleared out by the Hunt Authorities, and perhaps even recommended to Hunters as a location to which their prey might be directed by a former participant with a chip on her shoulder. In any case, Mara needed to be careful about what she said. On several occasions, she thought visitors were deliberately encouraging her to denounce the government, and though these suspicions were probably without substance, she resisted the temptation to express her feelings. There didn't seem to be any actual laws against what she was doing, but both of the Hunt advice websites she'd created mysteriously vanished a few seconds after appearing online, so it was clear that the authorities wanted to suppress as much information as possible.

Mara was also contacted by women she'd met during the Hunt, including several whose names she'd not heard before. All their messages struck much the same tone: they thanked Mara for her help, and expressed sadness about Julie. Some went into detail about what had been done to them, and how they were coping with what was officially known as 'post-Hunt trauma'. Even Anne got in touch, saying how guilty she felt about her good luck. Mara never heard from the other standby, but with the exception of Isabella, who presumably didn't have Internet access in prison, she eventually received emails from everyone who had been with her in the arena. Everyone who was still alive, that is.

The most curious thing that happened during this period was the arrival of a large package with no return address at Mara's apartment. It contained a painting of a woman's face, grotesquely distorted, yet radiating energy and defiance. It was obviously by the artist responsible for the paintings in Claire Richardson's house, presumably Claire herself. Mara didn't know what to make of this gift, but she liked the painting, and hung it in a prominent position on her living room wall. The first time Yuke set eyes on it, she gasped and said, "Mara! Who did this amazing portrait of you?" Mara looked at the picture again. How could she not have recognised the face as her own? It seemed so obvious now. And Claire must have painted her from memory! Mara emailed Claire thanking her profusely and suggesting they get together for a drink, but she never received a reply.

Yuke's career had blossomed. She'd been asked to write a regular column entitled "Le monde de Yuke" for the prestigious magazine *La passion pour le cinéma*, and was currently learning French so she wouldn't have to rely on a translator. The lease on her East Finchley apartment was about to expire, and now her financial situation had improved, she was determined to find a place closer to Mara, so they could see each other more often. Mara remained cautious: she treasured every minute spent with Yuke, but feared the consequences of being observed constantly entering and leaving each other's homes.

Her own writing wasn't going so well, work on *A Kill is Just a Kill* having ground to a halt. Mara thought she'd at least know how to conclude the book once Price's trial was over. But the trial provided no sense of closure.

This was not a story with a dramatic ending, a happy ending, or even a satisfyingly downbeat ending. By October, she had to admit the book was dead in the water, and could not be salvaged. This meant that, for the first time since the series began, there would be no Melissa Valance novel published the following year. Her publisher was more than understanding, and insisted Mara deserved a break. Mara's savings were substantial, so the prospect of making less money didn't worry her. On the other hand...

She had an idea. And the more she thought about it, the more convinced she became of its brilliance.

When Yuke arrived that Friday, Mara led her into the living room and said, "We need to discuss something important."

Yuke looked at Mara with concern. "What is it, honey?"

"The book I've been writing just isn't working, so I'm going to scrap it. That means I won't have anything published next year, and I'll need to start economising. I've been thinking about the best way of bringing in some additional income, and I've decided to rent out my guest bedroom."

The reality of what this meant was not lost on Yuke. Her face fell as she said, "I guess we'll have to be more careful about seeing each other from now on. But you can always visit me, and maybe somebody we trust will rent the room."

Mara could barely keep herself from grinning as she said, "Perhaps you know someone who'd be interested in renting a room."

Yuke frowned. "I could ask around, but I can't think of anyone offhand."

"Ideally, I'd be looking for an unattached female of approximately my own age."

Yuke could see Mara was getting at something. "Okay," she said uncertainly.

"And of course, I'd only be taking on a lodger because I need some extra money."

"Yes," said Yuke, more confused than ever.

"And not because I'd expect her to eat my pussy on a daily basis."

An enormous smile appeared on Yuke's face as she realised what Mara had in mind. "Do you really think it's possible?"

"It's perfect. People take in lodgers all the time, so nobody would think it unusual if you were living here. I even have a legitimate reason for suddenly deciding to rent a room."

Yuke could barely contain her joy. "When should I start moving my things over?"

"Right away. The room is bigger than your entire apartment, so there'll be plenty of space. And the bed is in good condition. Not that you'll be using it."

Yuke jumped onto Mara and began kissing her passionately. Neither woman needed to mention that by living together, they'd have an opportunity to explore their possibly unique connection, and arrive at a better understanding of its nature. Perhaps they would even discover its ultimate purpose. And what if it wasn't unique? What if other women had formed similar bonds? Here was a potential source of tremendous power, just waiting to be tapped. Britain's rulers had been using fear as a weapon long enough. Something like this might make them experience the emotion they'd so frequently inspired in others.

Mara spent the next few days supervising the carpenter who was installing wall-to-wall shelves in her guest room, and wondering how she could reconnect with Melissa Valance. Perhaps a less thematically ambitious Melissa adventure would recharge her creative batteries. But that was for later. Her Hunt novel may have been abandoned, but her intention of writing about the Hunt had not. Mara knew she wouldn't be good for anything until she'd written the Hunt out of her system. The general public now had more information about the Hunt than ever before, and if their understanding of this information was inevitably coloured by the right-wing press, there had to be people who were shocked and appalled by the details which had emerged. But the real impetus for change would surely come from elsewhere. South Africa's apartheid system only ended because of international sanctions that threatened to wreck the country's economy. Similar sanctions directed against the U.K. could bring about an end to the Hunt, and perhaps many of the other restrictions British women had to deal with.

Mara recalled telling Catherine about the Japanese saying: *Deru kui wa utareru.* The nail that sticks out gets hammered down. She'd compared herself to the nail. But now she would be the hammer. She would write a book telling the world what was going on in Great Britain, a book about her own experience. Not a thriller with a fictional protagonist, but an autobiography which would be more terrifying than any horror novel. She thought back to the evening before the letter from Hunt Administration arrived. She'd gone with Yuke to see *Heaven's Gate*, a film whose protagonist only makes a decisive stand against oppression when it's too late to do any good. Mara had waited a long time to take her own stand, but she didn't think it was too late. The Hunt had finally relaxed its grip on her, but she refused to relax her grip on it. She now understood that, for better or worse, her life was divided into three stages: before, during and after the Hunt. And that was how her book would be structured. She sat down in front of her computer and created a new file entitled *The Hunt*. At the top of page one, she wrote, "In Memory of J." If nothing else, she was determined to set the story straight about Julie. But this would also be another book for Yuke, a book which, if it had the desired effect, would ensure Yuke and thousands of women like her never had to go through the ordeal of the Hunt. Mara could not write this book without being totally truthful. Of course, she'd have to eliminate all references to her lover before sending the manuscript to a publisher. But for now, she would tell her story exactly as it happened, and let the unexpurgated draft sit on a shelf until the time was right.

Mara began writing in the first person, but soon realised this was the wrong approach. Direct narration would make the book unbearable, whereas, by referring to herself in the third person, she'd achieve just enough distance. Under the heading, "Book 1: Mara Gorki (Before the Hunt)," she wrote: "Mara hadn't left the apartment in almost a fortnight. She'd been writing a new Melissa Valance novel, potentially her best yet, and saw little reason to venture outside. Food could be ordered online or by phone, while Yuke's weekly visits satisfied her desires for sex and companionship. She wouldn't have described herself as agoraphobic, but staying home gave her a sense of security."

It was a good opening. While struggling with *A Kill is Just a Kill*, Mara feared the ability to write had permanently deserted her. But now she worked continuously for the rest of the day and throughout the night, stopping only when her eyes refused to remain open a minute longer, collapsing into bed as the light of a new morning appeared. She thought of Yuke, of Mary, of Claire, of Catherine, of Madeleine, of Julie. And once again, she dreamed of a familiar voice telling her to wake up. For a moment, Mara knew whose voice it was. Then the knowledge vanished, like smoke in the wind.

THE END

ABOUT THE AUTHOR

Brad Stevens is a film critic based in the UK. He is the author of *Monte Hellman: His Life and Films* (McFarland, 2003) and *Abel Ferrara: The Moral Vision* (FAB Press, 2004). His Bradlands column appears every month on Sight & Sound's website. He has also contributed to many film magazines, and works for several DVD/Blu-ray distributors. *The Hunt* is his first novel.